IMPULSIVE

IN A SMALL TOWN

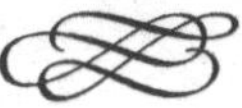

ALIE GARNETT

For my Family

AUTHOR'S NOTE

Author's note:

Before you start Impulsive about Sam and Natalie, I want to take a moment to tell you that if you haven't read the Hart Sisters series or, more importantly, Max Valentine is Looking at Me, you will want to read that first since Natalie and Sam head to Bitch Cove in order for Natalie to meet her birth mom. Natalie is the daughter she was forced to put up for adoption at birth. Now that baby is all grown up and going to leave one small town for another, falling in love along the way.

Download Max Valentine is Looking at Me today!

CHAPTER 1

WERE you actually supposed to have a panic attack on your wedding day?

Could you change out your wedding party on the day of your wedding?

Could you just call it off if someone you wanted to be there wasn't?

What if it rained?

What if all that happened all at once? Then could you just call it off?

Natalie Beckett had no answers to all the questions running through her head. Unfortunately, the answers were all she could think about. And she wanted them instantly. Should she have looked into them yesterday? Last week? Last month? Any day but today, because today was her actual wedding day.

It had taken close to a year of planning to get to this moment. Hours of her time and a lot of her dad's money. That time and money didn't change the fact that it suddenly all felt so wrong. Every single part of it.

Across the room, the bridesmaids were waiting out the last moments before the wedding, chatting in the corner with smiles and excitement. Without her. Weren't they supposed to be her closest friends? Because if they were, she would want to talk to one of them. Any of them. But they weren't her closest friends—not anymore, at least. Sure, two were Jason's sisters, so maybe not exactly her closest friends ever, but the third was her best friend from college, and either she had changed, or Natalie had. Natalie was worried it was herself— she didn't feel different.

Reaching up, she touched the elaborate hairdo that had her black wavy hair constrained into a ball on her head, with a few strands left free to hang around her face in little curls. Her fingers said that it was still perfect, that everything on the outside was perfect—everything but inside, Natalie herself. There was nothing perfect there.

In a flurry of pink, her friend Mia Lawson rushed across the room, pushing Natalie into the back room she had just gotten dressed in. Letting it happen, Natalie was relieved to see her return. Mia, at least, was a true friend. "The groom is coming down," she said, explaining why the separate room was needed as she shut the door behind them. Once it was closed, she turned and looked Natalie up and down. "The book club is here. Don't worry about it. They're all upstairs, waiting and excited to enjoy your big day. Oh, and it is hot up there. *Hot.* You're going to die in that dress. How many layers is it anyway?"

Natalie hugged the woman who she had asked to be her personal attendant a few months before when her supposed friend said she couldn't cancel some trip with her boyfriend. Mia had jumped at the opportunity. She had actually done this so many times in her almost thirty years that it was second nature to the bubbly woman. On the other hand, Natalie had never been in a wedding before, and now she was in her own and a little freaked out.

Looking down at the bouncy woman, Natalie bit her lip. Could she ask another favor of the woman? Mia was a relatively new friend, though they had known of each other for years. Mia was a waitress, and Natalie was the librarian at the public library in the same small town, but they had both joined a book club and had become actual friends in the last six months. Close considering the six-year age difference, but from the outside, they had little in common. However, the more they got to know each other, the more Natalie wasn't too sure about that. It was the same with everyone in the book club. They all were a little alike.

"Say it." Mia rolled her eyes as she jumped up and sat on the only furniture in the room, a craft table that sat against the wall. The move proved she had no concern for her pink dress that showed off her curves or what she looked like sitting on the table.

It was one of the reasons Natalie loved her. Mia didn't care what anyone thought, ever.

"Are you sure Hazel is here? She wasn't at the rehearsal dinner last night." Natalie bit her lip. Hazel was one of her oldest friends—if you could have old friends at twenty-three. They had gone through twelve grades of school together, and the graduating class was only twenty-seven, so they couldn't miss each other. But all through that time, Hazel had not been her best friend. Her best friend had been Hanna.

Hanna May had been Hazel's identical twin sister. They looked so much alike that Natalie sometimes couldn't say her name because it hurt so much to remember her best friend was gone. That in her place was just a replica. That in itself made Natalie hurt even more. Hazel had lived in her sister's shadow right up until Hanna died. And that had continued after her death.

For some reason, she needed Hazel here today. Natalie had only invited her two months before, even though she had sent out the rest of the invites mid-March, and it was late July now. They had become close in the last few months, sometimes laughing and talking like the old days. Natalie loved that it was possible they could be friends again. Now, as the hour arrived, she needed her there today more than anyone else.

Until last week she wouldn't have wondered if Hazel was there or not. That was when Natalie had asked Hazel to talk in private about her being gone on her honeymoon. Hazel had a panic attack, the worst one Natalie had ever seen. The other woman had run off in a blind panic and had ended up in the middle of the street being held by their pastor, unable to breathe. At that point, Natalie hadn't been able to handle the fact that she could cause that kind of reaction from one of her closest friends just by being near her.

She closed her eyes to try to stop the tears. It was her wedding day. No tears. But the memory of Hazel's reaction reminded her of all that was lost. Trying not to go to that alternate reality that the two groom's sisters were Hazel and Hanna and the groom was their brother Henry. It had been almost six years since that dream died on a back-country road, but it was still in her mind.

"Don't cry." Mia pulled a tissue from the bodice of her dress and handed it to her. "Hazel is here. She brought John Henry. They are here."

Natalie breathed deeply, trying to ward off the tears. Hazel almost always was with her four-year-old son, so today would be no different. The only time she was without him was during book club—it was no place for a little boy. The topic was always grizzly, horrifying murder. Adults only.

"Is it too late to have her as a bridesmaid?" Natalie wondered out loud.

"Yes," Mia stated. "Maybe she couldn't get anyone to watch John Henry? She doesn't always like to bring him to things."

"Maybe." But Natalie also knew Hazel didn't like to go to things and used her son as an excuse more than anything. It was her excuse the night before for missing the groom's supper. Fake or not, Natalie didn't know.

"And Mandy, Tess, and Ruth?" She named the others in the book club, which met every two weeks. Three women who, a few months ago, she had barely known but were now her closest friends.

"All are here," Mia assured her.

"Can you get married if it floods?" She looked out the little window where the rain was coming down in sheets. Mia seemed to actually have all the answers to Natalie's questions, which was why she was the perfect personal attendant.

"It won't flood, Natalie. Well, it would take more than this to flood." They were in North Dakota and near enough to the Red River that it did flood almost every year. But not usually from rain, just from winter snowmelt.

"We're going on a honeymoon, a beach honeymoon," Natalie stated out of nowhere. It wasn't even something she was worried about today, just every day up to today. It had been her main concern for weeks.

"Sounds fun," Mia said.

"It might be, I don't know. I didn't find a swimming suit that covered all my scars." Most of her body except her face and legs had scars from the car accident when she was seventeen, the accident she was not supposed to have survived.

"Do you have to cover the scars? They're a part of you." Mia leaned back on her hands and looked at Natalie.

The scars were something she never talked about. All her new friends knew about the accident—that was the good part of living in a small town. It had been up to Natalie to talk about it, and so far, she hadn't. With Hazel there, she wouldn't. Her pain from the accident would never match Hazel's.

"Jason doesn't like them. But the ones you can't see when I'm dressed are a lot worse. I quit getting the surgeries that would clean them up, make them look better. I was tired of being in pain." Natalie touched the unusually high neckline of her wedding dress, high enough to cover the scars.

"Those scars prove that you are a fighter and can make it through anything." Mia put a positive spin on it. She was way more positive than Natalie, but Natalie lived with a spattering of scars while Mia's body was still perfect.

Over the last few months, Jason had started hinting about Natalie going in to try to correct more of the scars. Just the ones he deemed 'upsetting.' Mostly, she had ignored him when he said it, but when they were married, she was worried his opinion was going to have her back in surgeries she didn't want. But she knew how she was with peer pressure, even if she hated it.

"Tell me some gossip," Natalie demanded of her friend, wanting to change the topic. That usually was not a problem with Mia, who worked at the café she owned almost every day and talked to just about everyone in town. Landstad had around 1500 people living in it, and Mia knew everything about everyone. The woman had a personality that made everyone feel special in her presence and loosened lips easily.

"About anyone in particular?" Mia asked.

"Anyone. Well, maybe someone I know." Not that there were many people in Landstad she didn't know.

"You cannot tell anyone. Not even your husband or the book club." Mia demanded loyalty. Which only meant that the gossip was exceptionally good. Mia was a gossip, but she could keep a secret when needed.

"Okay," Natalie whispered, hoping she could keep the promise.

"Nobody, Natalie. It never leaves this room," Mia said again as she moved closer.

"Jesus, Mia, if it's that much of a secret, maybe tell me something else." Natalie looked at the clock on the wall in front of her, wishing time would slow or speed up—whichever made her stomach stop twisting. The clock only mocked her by telling her it was 10:05 a.m. Broken.

"Fine. Okay. I took Hazel home last week after her panic attack, and we talked for a long time. She has the hots for our minister." The three of them actually went to the same church every Sunday. This church, to be exact.

Looking up at the ceiling, she smiled for the first time in what felt like a lifetime. The minister was young and hot but not her type at all. He was totally Hazel's type, though. "Pastor Ruston?"

"Yup. But she is having some problems with religion right now and doesn't see a future with him." Mia shrugged.

"What about him?" Natalie had almost forgotten about her wedding. It would have to wait until Mia was done with her story. This was good.

"I don't know how he feels, but from his reaction to her last week, I would say he is just as interested. Now the biggest secret is that Hazel went to a party over the summer and ran into him. Like a college party with drinking and drugs and … well, a college party. So, they ended up having sex at a party. Like, at the party." Mia said sex in a whisper. Probably because they were in a church.

"Holy crap." Little mild-mannered Hazel and their sexy pastor getting busy at a party. Natalie couldn't even see that happening.

Some of Natalie's earliest memories were of the May twins, and Hazel had always been the shy one compared to Hanna's outgoing nature. From kindergarten onward, Hazel had been quiet and in the background the entire time. Even when they had partied together in high school, Hazel had been the sober one, the somber one, the disapproving one. Though she had a son out of wedlock, she hadn't changed as far as Natalie could tell. But maybe Natalie wasn't noticing enough about her old friend.

"No kidding. And now you get to walk up the aisle and look into his face. You will have to spend your entire wedding thinking about him and Hazy getting busy." Mia laughed at Natalie's expression of horror.

"Holy crap, Hazel is going to Hell." Natalie slammed her hand to her mouth, then added in sudden fear, "Holy crap, I have to get married."

"Hazel will be fine. They both need a little shaking up. And I think it did the trick. And you do not have to get married."

"Of course, I have to get married. Everybody is here expecting me to get married in a few minutes." She gestured above them at all the people she knew were there because she had invited them. Addressed every envelope, then counted and recounted the RSVPs.

"Doesn't mean you have to get married. The most important person here is you. If you want to ditch this party, you can." Mia jumped off the table.

"What about my dad?" Natalie was warming to the idea but didn't want to hurt her dad. He, after all, had been looking forward to today just as much as she had.

"He'll be just fine. You have put him through a lot more crap than a ditched wedding," Mia pointed out.

Natalie knew she had been hard to raise for the single father whose wife died not long after their only child had started kinder-garten. Looking back on it, she could see she had been wild and uncontrollable for many years. Through it all, her dad had never wavered in his love for her. He never let on that it had been a challenge.

"I cannot just walk through the church and walk out." For sure, someone would notice. Would someone actually stop her?

"You'll have to go out the window," Mia said, and both turned to look at the window. It was a small window.

Natalie was sure that the window was painted shut and had been for years; she had never seen it open. And it was small, no bigger than any other basement window she had seen in her life. She and her bulky dress were not ever getting out of that window.

"It's too small," Natalie whispered in disappointment.

"When I was in confirmation, my entire class climbed out that window, including Stephanie Willis, and she was always as big as she is today," Mia said of a friendly woman who came into the library a few times a month with her four noisy kids. If she could fit through that window, Natalie was sure she could.

"Do you think I can?" Natalie asked more about leaving than if she could fit.

"Better to leave now than after."

Natalie smelled the roses in her bouquet; they were fake, but Faith Champ had somehow made them smell real. Faith had spent months working on these for her. She was the art teacher at the high school with her dad, who taught science. They had been friends forever.

Setting down the flowers on the table, she looked at Mia. "I have to get out of here."

Mia smiled back at her. "Out the window, and then I will stall the wedding for twenty minutes. My Jeep is in the parking lot. The keys are in it."

Natalie hitched up her beautiful large white dress and climbed onto the table. For some reason, Natalie couldn't stop smiling. All the weight lifting from her made anything possible right in that moment.

Mia put her hand on her leg and pulled a phone from between her ample breasts, placing it in Natalie's hand. "You'll need this. Call when you land."

Natalie took the phone and stood up on the table, pushed up the window, and easily climbed out of it. Too easily for how small it was. She went out headfirst with Mia pushing her dress out as she went. She was free.

Within an instant, she was completely soaked from the sheets of rain coming from the sky. Jumping to her feet, she blindly ran toward the back of the parking lot, where she saw Mia's red Jeep waiting for her. All she had to do was run through three large puddles and a torrent of rain. She could do this. She had to. She couldn't go back now.

She was almost there when someone came out from behind a black pickup truck right into her path. Putting her hands up, she was just going to tackle the person like she had been taught in high school Physical Ed class. Praying it wasn't an old person because she wasn't stopping, she put her weight into the tackle like she was taught.

Just as she made contact, she felt herself being lifted off the ground. At that point, she knew she was never getting to Mia's Jeep.

CHAPTER 2

The runaway bride was in Sam Sullivan's arms before he even knew what he was doing. What was he doing? It seemed like she had a plan, so just let her go and do her thing. She didn't need him.

Even with a soaking wet dress, she was easy to sweep into his arms. Too easy.

Sam had been sitting in his truck waiting for the rain to let up a little before he went into the church. The day was here, and he was not excited to attend the wedding. He was actually only here so he could tell Patrick that he had gone. Weddings were not his thing.

Moments before seeing her, he had actually decided that he was not going inside with the rain coming down like it was. There was no way he was sitting through the wedding, miserable and wet. But then he had seen it, a blur of white by the back of the church heading his way. He jumped out of the truck and headed her off as she ran for the back of the parking lot.

"Get me out of here," she hissed from his arms.

Spinning around, he carried her to his truck and opened the passenger door. After letting her climb in, he rushed around the car to the driver's side and, without a word, started it and backed out of the spot and then out of the parking lot. Pulling onto Main Street, they sped away from the little white church as fast as he could go. At least he wouldn't have to go to a wedding anymore.

"Where to?"

"I have no idea." She was trying to fix the ball of wet hair on her head, but nothing helped.

Natalie Beckett was as beautiful as she had been on the wedding announcement he had placed on his fridge months ago. He looked at that photo every day. Long black hair, wavy and thick, with dark green eyes that sparkled with happiness. Perfect, almost flawless olive skin. This beautiful woman looked nothing like the little trouble-making teen who had made the first few months of his first year of teaching unbearable.

"My place?" It felt odd asking the bride back to his place. Sounded like a come on.

"Where do you live?" Since it was a small town, she would know almost every house in it.

"Behind your dad," he answered.

"The Jackson or Knutson place?" Of course, she'd know the previous owners; she had grown up in the house her father still lived in. He thought she had moved back in with her dad when she was done with college, but he hadn't seen her. The subject hadn't come up, and he hadn't asked Patrick. It wasn't for him to know.

"Jackson, I think. The blue one." He tried to remember what he had been told years before when he had purchased the place. At the time, he hadn't even realized it was so close to his friend's house, just across the back yard. Now they didn't usually get together at home either—they worked together.

"Yeah, that was Beth Jackson's house. Did she ever marry Todd? I can go there and then just walk home." She turned to look out the window. So much for her telling him why she ditched her wedding. Not that it mattered, that was her business.

Nodding, he knew she wasn't looking for an answer as he drove the short distance. Pulling into his garage to get out of the rain, he closed the garage door. He could tell she didn't want anyone to know where she was. Both soaking wet when they walked into the main part of the house, they kicked off their shoes but still dripped water everywhere.

Sam looked at his new light tan carpet and said, "I'll close my eyes, and you can get out of your dress and go take a shower. I'll bring you clothes when I get out of my wet stuff." It sounded like a decent plan.

"Okay, but I can't get out of this dress alone. Can you do the buttons and stuff on the back?" She turned her back to him.

Taking a breath, he looked up at her, all smooth olive skin in contrast to the white dress she wore. It was a tight dress and took some strength to get the first few buttons undone. He tried not to touch her bare skin, but it was impossible with the tiny buttons. Her skin was as smooth and soft as it looked. Each button revealed more and more of her perfect back until he got to about the fifth one, then fine white lines started to appear.

Button after button revealed more scars. His heart hurt as they became more numerous and obvious. After a few more buttons, he couldn't stop himself from lightly touching one of the lines with his finger to see how it felt.

She flinched and turned away from him. "Sorry, skin graft scars," she explained. Not that he didn't know all about her surgeries; Patrick had kept him informed as it had been happening. Surgery after surgery.

"No need to apologize. I'm sorry. I shouldn't have touched them." He wished he had been strong enough not to need to touch them. Feel how real they were.

"Too many not to, right? Now close your eyes." Her words were filled with sadness.

"Okay." He closed his eyes with regret.

He could tell by her reaction that the scars bothered her. Didn't she know by now it was the scars that made people more interesting? Some have scars that show, some don't. Natalie had spent a year in Hell to get those scars. She shouldn't be ashamed of them.

Listening to her quietly walk across his living room, he wondered if she was naked. Which made him picture her naked, which he shouldn't. She had been his student, he reminded himself as he took off his shirt while keeping his eyes closed. Dropping it on the floor then pulling his T-shirt off, he wondered if she was in the bathroom yet. He hadn't heard the door close.

"Looking good, sexy Sam. I'm gone." With a laugh as enticing as it had been years before, she called him the nickname she had given him his first day of teaching history at Landstad High School, a nickname he sometimes still got called. She was still annoying.

After opening his eyes to make sure she was gone, he peeled off his wet jeans and left them in a pile on the ground with her dress. Along with a white, lacy strapless bra and a scrap of underwear that made him realize she had been completely naked when she walked through the room.

He pulled off his socks but left his underwear on in case she came out before he could get to his bedroom, not at all because he wanted to hide how her being naked in his house had affected him. Walking down the hall, he didn't hear the shower running in the guest bathroom, but as he entered his master bedroom, he heard the shower running.

She was naked in his shower. Natalie Beckett was naked in his shower, using his soap on her tall, sexy body. And he was standing in the middle of his bedroom with a full-on erection for one of his former students. This wasn't how he thought this day would ever go.

He needed to get his mind off naked women, or at least this naked woman. Finding sweats and T-shirts for them both, he slid a set into the bathroom for her and then closed the door again. But the hot steamy air that had escaped the room smelled like her—vanilla and citrus—making him think of senior history.

By the time she came out of the bathroom, he was in the living room sitting on the couch, flipping through channels. The wet clothes were stuffed into his laundry room since he had no idea what to do with them. It had taken time to get his body back under control. Dealing with a muddy, wet wedding dress helped.

How she managed to make a baggy orange Landstad Tigers T-shirt and oversized black sweatpants look so good, he didn't know. Her hair ran down her back in long black waves, still wet from her shower. Her bright green eyes were less wary than they had been on the drive over.

Slumping down onto the other end of the couch from him, she said, "Thank you for saving me, Mr. Sullivan. I just needed to get away from there."

"I just did what anyone would have done. Damsel in distress and all." He smiled at her.

"I guess I did need saving." The phone rang in her hand, and without looking at it, she hit a button, shutting the sound shut off. It rang again.

"You should call your dad." He watched her glance at the phone again and ignore another call.

She cringed as she said, "No, he is going to be so mad."

"No, he would like to know that you are okay. Patrick has never been mad at you. You can do no wrong in his eyes." Sam told her the truth of what he had seen of his friend over the years. Natalie had made some big mistakes, and Patrick would just let it go. 'It's Natalie,' was his favorite saying.

"Usually, but this is maybe too much, even for Perfect Patrick." She read a text that had come in.

"Perfect Patrick?" His eyebrow raised.

"Mom used to call him that. I always thought it was cute that she called him out on his non-faults. She wasn't there today." Natalie put her phone down on the coffee table and looked out the window; the rain had finally stopped, but the day was still dreary beyond the glass.

"I bet your dad had his camera out recording the day for her." Sam reached out and put a hand on her shoulder in comfort and squeezed.

Every event in Natalie's life had been captured by her father's video camera. All for her mom to see one day. Though the woman had died years before Sam came to town, he knew all videos started with her dad saying, "Look, Mom, look at Natalie today." From ball games she had played to big and small events in her life. Sam had seen a few of them after the accident, but he hadn't seen many since then.

"He did. Making everyone crazy as he videoed it all." A small smile spread over her lips.

"Just text him. He just wants to know you're okay." He wanted to reach over and comfort her but didn't.

"Fine." She picked up her phone and typed for a while.

Looking at the TV, he asked, "Do you want to watch this?"

She didn't look up as she said, "Yeah, it's okay."

They watched the end of the movie he had seen twenty times as she sent out texts. Her lower lip was permanently between her teeth as she typed, and every once in a while, a sound would indicate that she was getting a new text.

"Dad asked if I could stay here tonight. Jason is looking for me. I should talk to him, but I'm not ready. I don't know what to say yet." She looked up at him.

"Sure. The spare room is all ready for you. Did you want to sneak home and get some stuff?"

"No, I think I'll wait until tomorrow. Maybe let things settle down a little. I have to make a plan for my life. Tomorrow maybe."

"I don't know if you need an entirely new plan for life. You have your job at the library. Your dad isn't kicking you out. Just keep going like before." He didn't notice the new movie that started in front of them. All his attention was on her.

"I was moving to Fargo, so I turned in my notice at the library. Dad has to be tired of me."

"Your dad has never been tired of you. You're the center of his life. I didn't really know if he was actually going to let you get married today. I had figured he would throw you over his shoulder and carry you out of the church long before letting you get married." He chuckled and was happy when she joined in with a big laugh.

"I would crush him," she admitted, settling into the couch more.

Even though she wasn't all that big around, she was just under six feet tall, and her father was closer to 5'5". She had been taller than her father for as long as Sam had known them. It dawned on Sam that she didn't look like him either—Patrick was a blond-haired, blue-eyed, stocky man, and his daughter was tall, slim, and dark.

"He would let you. You do nothing wrong, Natalie."

"Quit saying that, Mr. Sullivan. It makes me feel like I take advantage of him." She groaned.

"Call me Sam."

"Can I call you sexy Sam?" Her green eyes sparkled.

"No. And I wish you'd never made that one up."

"Hanna made it up, not me. I just said it more. Mostly to your face." Laughing, she pulled her feet under her and turned toward him, leaning her head against the back of the couch.

"It was super annoying. It made my first year teaching hard," he confessed.

"I was pretty mean to you," she admitted easily.

He turned toward her. "You were."

"Sorry." She crinkled her nose.

"I've gotten over it. Mostly," he informed her with a laugh.

"What was the worst thing I did?"

He had always wondered if her memory had been affected by the accident but had never dared ask Patrick about it. "I think it was the May sisters boob thing. Not very nice thing to do to a young guy." He watched her eyes sparkle again at the memory.

It had been early fall in his first year teaching history, and the three girls had come into his classroom during lunch. Just the three, Natalie and the twins, Hanna and Hazel May. They had started to talk to him about how they were twins and that they were identical, and that meant everything about them should be identical. He had taken the conversation seriously and argued that even twins have differences. And out of the blue, Natalie stated that the twins' breasts were not the exact same and he needed to look to see if there was a difference the three of them couldn't see. Before he could stop them, both the twins raised their shirts and showed him their bare breasts. He had been twenty-four at the time, and sex was still foremost in his mind. There he was staring at four breasts that were actually identical.

The girls ran out of the classroom laughing, and Sam was stuck picturing those two girls' breasts every time he looked at them for months. The worst part of the entire incident was that as he looked at the perky breasts, he really wanted to see Natalie's, not the twins.

"I forgot that. That was fun. I miss those days." Her voice was soft and dreamy.

"I don't," Sam said with a smile, but she didn't respond back with one.

"I stood there today in my wedding dress imagining I was marrying Henry. That Hazel and Hanna were my bridesmaids. That that day had never happened. I wanted it to be true so bad. I had Mia make sure that Hazel was there today. I couldn't get married without her there. But I wanted them all there. I miss them." Tears started running down her face.

Sam reached over and pulled her into his arms. Maybe that was why he hadn't wanted to go to the wedding, because he would look for them too. The four of them had been together all the time until the accident. When he had first heard that there were four in the car, he was convinced he knew who they all were. He was sure the triplets had all been there, not Hanna's new boyfriend. That they were all gone.

Letting her cry, he ran his hand over the wet, black curly hair that hung down her back, letting his mind go back to the day he was convinced he would never teach again. Ever. The day he would never forget.

When he had moved to Landstad, he had been asked to join the volunteer firefighters. Wanting to be involved in his new community made him jump at the idea. There had been nothing big but grass fires until early November. He was up in his apartment downtown when the call came through. A car accident not far from town. He was closest, so he got there before almost anyone else. A single car had rolled, ejecting all of the passengers.

At the time, he had never dealt with that kind of scene. He wasn't prepared for it. The couple whose yard the accident had happened in were both EMTs, and Natalie wouldn't be alive had it not been for those two.

When he arrived, the couple had car headlights flashing over the scene. The wife called him over as she was working on Natalie, blood everywhere. The woman was shoving a tube down her throat. She was unrecognizable except for the letterman's jacket she wore that said Henry on it. It was Natalie. She had worn that coat since the cold weather of fall had set in.

After being instructed to do chest compressions, he started and looked around the yard. The husband had come back to them and said the rest were gone—three others. In his mind, he knew Henry was one of them. He knew Hanna was probably another one. He was sure that Hazel was the fourth. They were always together. Always. He was glad for the darkness, so he couldn't see the others. Natalie had been enough.

It had taken too long for the ambulance to show up. They were not that far from town. More firefighters came, and more headlights illuminated the scene, something Sam would never get out of his mind.

Though the ambulance came, it wasn't until he heard a helicopter approach that they started talking about moving her. Natalie was being airlifted to the hospital. He knew she needed to be.

As he did his compressions, he tried not to touch the large piece of glass sticking out of her stomach. The rule was that you left it in, and doctors would remove it. But all he wanted to do was take it out—it had to be hurting her. But his hands had to do the compressions to keep her heart beating.

The helicopter landed, with more lights and EMTs flooding out of the machine and swarming him. Pushing him aside, they took over and got her on a stretcher and into the helicopter. From his spot on the ground, he watched it go up in the air and head south. He ran his hands through his hair, not caring that they were covered in blood. Was she already dead? Would she be dead by morning? Would her dad get to see her one more time before she died?

Unable to move from the spot that held so much of her blood, he went into shock. He looked around the yard as the EMTs and firefighters loaded a body into an ambulance with no sirens on. No rush for the dead. He knew that was one of his students, no matter which one it was.

One of his firefighting buddies came to him and asked if he was okay. Sam asked who the others were. All names were what he thought until his friend said Jamie Smith, not Hazel. It was like God had given him back Hazel. Like he couldn't take all three of the triplets in one night.

Sam had made it home but was still in a daze. There was so much of Natalie's blood on him that when he had taken a shower, the water ran red for a while. He silently wept, letting his tears run for the kids who had lost their lives in a single moment. All were in the senior class, and half were siblings. Until that moment, he had never thought life could be so cruel.

Natalie had lived through the night, then through the next day, then a week. Four months later, she woke up from the coma. Patrick didn't come back to school until the following year since she was in the hospital until late in the summer. Then she didn't come back to Landstad but had stayed in Fargo due to extensive operations still needed and physical therapy.

When the new year began, he started to have lunch with Patrick and heard all about Natalie and her slow recovery. Since she had broken a dozen bones in her body, she had gone through many surgeries. The broken bones had healed before she had woken from the coma, but they hadn't wanted to do some of the surgeries until she woke up, so for two years, she had surgeries on and off. Around the Christmas after the accident, Patrick had taken a month off so that Natalie could have a complete facial reconstruction.

Through all that, she had to learn to live with the fact that three people had died that night—her boyfriend, her best friend, and another. The facts slowly came out about the accident, that the group was drunk and not wearing seat belts, speeding along the gravel roads.

The morning after the accident, Sam had quit the volunteer firefighters. He didn't stop at accidents when he saw them along the side of the road. Movies sometimes bothered him now. Every now and then, he would even have nightmares.

Natalie had stopped crying on his chest. Her breathing had smoothed out, and he wondered if she was asleep. The even breathing continued until the movie ended, but still, he rubbed her back and ran his hands over her hair. He was glad he had been able to rescue her today. A far easier rescue than years before.

CHAPTER 3

FAMILIAR PAIN WOKE NATALIE, dragging her from the sleep she hadn't been getting for days. But her back would never let her sleep too long in one position. It had been almost six years, it shouldn't bother her so much, but it still did now and them.

There was a body curled around hers, a body she knew wasn't Jason. Jason didn't like to touch when they were sleeping. Blinking into the dark, she realized it was Sam Sullivan, the sexy history teacher from her past.

How was she ever going to get up without waking him? Just because she was forced to get up didn't mean he needed to. Biting her lip against the pain, she sat up and stretched. Of course, the movement woke him up.

"Are you okay?" he mumbled, his eyes not even opening.

"I'm fine, I just need to move. My back sometimes bothers me." She got up and headed to the bathroom. The hallway one this time. When she had walked through the house naked, she hadn't noticed this one. Her mind couldn't get beyond Sam Sullivan's abs. Holy cow! Shouldn't teachers' bodies be less yummy than that? It caused her to miss the hallway bathroom completely, and she found herself in his bedroom. When she heard him start moving, she dashed into the closest bathroom. What must he think of her just using his shower?

After a few minutes of stretches, she knew she had to get her medicine. So, she needed to run home and get that. When she got back to the living room, he was curled on his side and fast asleep, so she pulled the blanket off the back of the couch and tucked it around him, smiling. It was the least she could do.

She slipped out of the house and walked through the backyard into her dad's backyard. It was almost dawn, so the town was quiet. Not even a dog barked. Her dad never locked the back door, so she easily got into her childhood home; one too many lost keys when she was younger had taught him to just leave it open. In the living room, she saw that her dad had taken off his suit there, so she picked up the white starched shirt from the floor and hung it on the back of a chair, then picked up his pants, wondering why he would even take them off in the living room. As she laid them on the chair that held his shirt, she noticed a blue pile on the floor. Picking it up, she saw it was a dress. Her dad did not wear dresses. Nor did he ever date. Not once since her mom had died.

She laid the dress over the chair and went to her room with a smile on her face. Her dad had gotten lucky. Good for him. He deserved to be happy again.

The suitcase she had packed for the honeymoon was there, still packed. Grabbing it, she knew everything she would need for a few days was in the bag. Then she went to her top dresser drawer and pulled out a small picture storage box. Taking the two items, she headed out of the house, hoping not to wake her dad or his friend.

Slipping back into Sam's house, she saw he was still sleeping, so she went to the spare bedroom and closed the door. She opened her bag and pulled out a pair of panties. No more going commando. Commando in someone else's pants. Sexy Sam's pants. Had he gone commando in them ever?

She bit her lip as heat pooled in her core at the thought. Quickly, she pulled on her panties, then she put the pants back on, even if she had her own clothes. She liked his. She knew she shouldn't think about him like that, but it was hard not to. He was hot. Ever since the first day she had seen him, she had thought so. Back then, it was just a silly teen crush, but now it could easily turn into a full-blown woman crush. He was so nice to look at. Not that she would ever act on it—he had been her teacher, after all. Granted, he hadn't been her teacher for almost six years, but in her mind, he was still lecturing her about history. Maybe she should tell him that the civil war has never come up in a conversation in her adult life.

Sitting on the bed, she felt better than she had in weeks. Everyone had asked if the wedding was stressing her out, but it wasn't the wedding; it was being married. There were things about Jason that bothered her. From little things, like his constant need to be right, to the big things, like how he didn't like her body. Looking back, she saw that the pieces were all in place for her to bail on her wedding.

If she had gotten married eight months before, she would have done it and been happy—for a while at least. But seven months ago, she had joined the book club. It had made her feel differently about the people in the little town she grew up in, a bit more accepting.

That early afternoon in January, she was supposed to have lunch with her dad after her morning shift at the library. But he had bailed for some reason, so she had eaten lunch alone at the café. Reading a book, she listened to the conversations around her. At that point, a name caught her ears: Ted Bundy. Who was talking about him in a small café in North Dakota?

In the booth behind her, two ladies were talking about starting a book club where they would read books on serial killers and then discuss it. When they discussed the time and place with Mia, the owner of the café, Natalie knew she would be crashing the event. She wanted in. Though she didn't know what book they were reading, she knew enough about him to bluff it.

Her lunch was disrupted, however, when she saw her ex-friend Hazel May walking down the aisle. Hazel, of course, looked at Natalie like she had just killed Hazel's puppy. Sadly, it was worse—she had killed her family. Lunch half-eaten, she threw down some money before anything happened with Hazel or her family.

It was the next day when she actually met everyone. Ruth Kennedy from the insurance office, who was five or six years older than Natalie, and Mia, who was about Ruth's age. Mia had invited her cousin Mandy Nordskov, who was the new nurse at the town's health clinic. The only actual stranger was the bank's new president, Tess Thorn. They were great ladies who shared an interest in serial killers. It had taken a lot of courage for Natalie to stay when one of the other people there was Hazel May. Mia had somehow put them at ease with alcohol, which had turned into a staple of their gatherings.

Now they got together every other week and talked about serial killers while drinking alcohol. But what actually happened was that the conversation was so good Natalie pushed the group to start recording the talks and release them as a podcast. After releasing a few, they started to get a following and were really enjoying what they were doing—even if Natalie had added more to her already busy plate by doing everything for the podcast.

But mostly Natalie had gained some great new friends, friends who, months before, she would have never had thought she would have anything in common with. Mia would rally the group to events. They had all been involved in the Red River Flood Fundraiser Auction in the spring and the fourth of July celebration. Natalie had Ruth do a book signing that everyone showed up to at the library, even Hazel and her son. And all but Hazel had shown up for Natalie's rehearsal dinner—they had more fun than she did.

She knew that they were all involved in Natalie leaving the church. Mia was in charge of the escape, but the other four would be involved in some way. That was what friends did. They were who should have been her bridesmaids.

Hazel's son was hard on Natalie, though she would never admit it to anyone. Her three-year-old looked just like Hazel, just like Henry. The twins had been identical, but their triplet brother looked the same. Just a boy. So that little boy whose name was John Henry always reminded her of what Henry's kids would have looked like. As long as they weren't with her. Her dark features would have dominated any kids they would have had together.

Over the past few weeks, melancholy had overtaken Natalie. From missing her lost friends to Hazel's meltdown just last week. She had wanted to see if Hazel wanted to learn the podcasting business so that when she was gone, Hazel could do it. But Hazel instead thought she was bringing up the past and had a full-blown panic attack. Mia had said that Pastor Ruston had caught her before she could drive away because she would have crashed if she was in a car.

What Hazel had said right before the attack still played in her mind. She had said that they had not been friends anymore when the accident happened and that she had always felt like a third wheel in their threesome. That she had been replaced by her own brother as the third wheel, leaving her behind. Natalie had looked back on her childhood and could actually see it in retrospect. They always had to bring Hazel along. Don't forget Hazel. Include Hazel. She had been a bad friend. Then Natalie had killed two of Hazel's threesome from birth. No wonder the woman hated her. Natalie hated herself for what she did.

All through getting ready for the wedding—hair, make-up, dressing—she had wanted to know if Hazel was there. Natalie wouldn't allow another event in her life to take place without Hazel there. Included. Wanted.

On top of all the Hazel and accident stuff, she had started to think about her mom. Her mom would miss the biggest day of her life. Another person who would miss this day because of Natalie. She watched her dad holding his video camera recording the entire event for "Mom." Sam had been wrong about her dad recording everything for her mom, who died of cancer when Natalie was six. Instead, her dad recorded everything for the woman who had given Natalie up for adoption at birth. The recordings from the very beginning were addressed to "Mom," but her mom had still been there when the films had started.

Was it wrong of her to have not contacted her birth mom? Natalie had gotten a letter from her years ago, but she was still enduring surgery after surgery. Patrick had made her write to the woman, just to tell her she was okay, but she didn't feel okay then. So, she had sent a letter and an old picture of herself from before the accident—there were no photos from after for many years. Even now she could look at a picture of herself and see all the work that had been done to make her look somewhat like she used to. But mostly, she looked completely different.

This week, for the first time in her life, she had searched the internet for information on the woman who had given her life. After the rehearsal dinner had ended and late into the night, she started looking again and thought that she had found something. The names matched, but that was all that matched. The picture that showed the woman with the name of her mother looked nothing like Natalie, except she had green eyes.

The sun was starting to come up, and Natalie wondered when Sam Sullivan was going to kick her out. She had been awful to him when she was in his class, but he had been so cute she had wanted him to notice her. Why? She had no idea.

He still wore his blond hair a little longer than he should, like he forgot to get his hair cut, and those dark brown eyes were forever looking at her in disappointment. Yesterday that disappointment was not there—they were nicer without it. Oddly, he was always only an inch or two taller than her. Taller, actually, since her back surgery had taken her height down an inch.

Looking away from the rising sun, she saw him, all wake-up-sexy and standing in the doorway. She watched him scan the room until his eyes rested on her. Natalie squirmed and forced herself not to compare him to the man she had almost married, a man who was not coming close to measuring up to the teacher.

He folded his arms. "You went home?"

"Yes. Dad had company, so I came back." She was trying not to smile.

"Faith," he stated with a nod.

"I only saw their clothes in the living room." She blushed a little at the thought of how they ended up there.

"Faith then," he said with confidence.

"How long has that been going on?" She needed to know. Sam

didn't make it sound recent. He made it sound like an ongoing thing, something everyone knew but her. Why wouldn't he have told her about it?

"Probably since before your accident." He lost his smile at the word.

"Why didn't he ever say?" she asked, but he wouldn't know. She needed to ask her dad about it.

"Maybe he thought you weren't ready for him to date?"

Looking back out the window, she wanted to yell back that she had always wanted her dad to date. To get married. To not focus all his attention on her. "He took off his wedding ring when I was fifteen. Just one day, it was gone. Mom had died just under ten years before. I wondered why he didn't keep it on until the tenth anniversary." She looked down at her own hands as she spoke. "But we never talked about it. I never even asked. I should have asked."

"Maybe he was ready then." He sat down on the bed against the pillow beside her. "Do you remember your mom?"

"Yes. I was six when she died. Breast cancer. She had it before I was born too, but it came back. That last year she spent mostly in bed. I would sit beside her and read to her. I was an early reader, so I could read pretty good by then." She was still looking at the trees outside the window. "Then she was gone, and I didn't understand what had happened. Dad cried a lot, so I cried a lot. That fall, I went to school for the first time and met Hanna and Hazel, and they didn't have a mom either. We bonded over that. Sad, really."

"Did she look like you?" Sam took her hand in his.

"No." She laughed. "If you met her, you would think that she was Hazel's mom. All light blonde and gray eyes, I think. Little, too, like Hazel. Maybe another reason I bonded with those two."

He was silent as he held her hand. Not asking, not prodding.

"I'm adopted. I don't tell people that." She answered the question he didn't ask.

"I've never heard your dad even hint that you were anything but his," Sam confessed.

"If you listen, he does. I am a gift, I was chosen, he doesn't deserve to have me … If you're not listening for it, you don't notice it." She turned away from the window and looked at where their hands were linked. "After the cancer, Mom couldn't have kids, but they both wanted kids. It took a few years before they got the call. Dad said Mom wouldn't have said no to any baby, but they loved me at first sight. I had a great life with them. I wouldn't change it for the world." Her free hand was caressing his that was holding hers.

"Have you ever looked for her?" Sam asked.

"Not until this last week. I started to think about not getting to see my daughter get married. Maybe she deserved to be there. I blame it on Dad. He's always making those videos. They're for my real mom, if I ever meet her, so she can see how thankful he was to have been able to raise me."

"Perfect Patrick," Sam said with a sad laugh.

"See, he is. And now he has been hiding his girlfriend from me." She wiped the tears from her eyes.

"Talk to him." He let go of her hand and got up. "I'm going to get my computer, and you can show me what you've found."

Pulling the covers over her legs, Natalie was surprised how nice it felt to be able to talk to someone about her real mom. She hadn't even told Jason about it. She hadn't felt as comfortable with him as she did with Sam. And after only a few hours.

Now she was going to see what Sam thought of the woman she had found.

CHAPTER 4

Sam grabbed his computer from the living room end table and headed back to the bedroom, taking calming breaths. Natalie's story had made him want to pull her into his arms to comfort her again, but her hand caressing his made him want to pull her into his arms for a completely different reason. A hotter reason. He cursed himself because she was supposed to be on her honeymoon right now with another guy.

She was your former student, he told himself. Why was it so hard for him to remember that with Natalie? It had never been an issue before, not since his first year in Landstad. But, of course, it was her who had been the issue then also.

Stopping in the doorway, he looked at the woman who had blown his mind with her revelation. Adopted. He had always assumed her mother had been a dark-haired, olive-skinned beauty. And oddly tall. But, in reality, being adopted made way more sense. Adoption had made Patrick lenient with her. She could do no wrong, and she was never any trouble. The man loved her like he could lose her, and adoption meant it was a possibility.

Since he had left to get the computer, she had pulled her long legs under the covers, disappointing him a little. But she was still sitting up in bed waiting for him. When she saw him, she smiled at him so innocently. All he wanted to do was crawl into bed with her and throw the computer against the wall as he pulled her underneath him, kissing her the entire time—and not innocently.

Inwardly cursing at his body's reaction, he climbed onto the bed next to her, hoping she wouldn't notice. Handing her the computer, he let her do the searching since she knew what she was looking for. He didn't watch what she typed, just watched her slender fingers moving gracefully across the keys.

"When I search her name, I get all these pages, but really they are all about the same person. Judge Delphinea Connor Hart. That's her name. Not Judge, of course. But she looks nothing like me. I had always thought she would." Natalie pointed to the screen.

Sam looked up from her agile fingers and saw a redhead in a black robe pictured on the screen. Natalie looked nothing like this picture, pre- or post-accident. Then he saw something, and it all became clear. Pulling the computer to him, he said, "You have her eyes. See the green with the sparkles? She's happy in this picture."

"What sparkles?" She looked at him with the same sparkles of amusement.

"Nothing. She also has your nose." He quickly tried to turn the conversation away from his slip-up.

"I don't see it." Natalie looked back at the screen.

"This is your expression, Natalie. I would tell you to study for a test, and this was the face you'd make. Smiling but actually saying 'fuck you.' Face turned up a little in defiance, covering it with a smile. This is your face." He turned the screen back to her.

He had seen that face almost every day from September first until the accident. Whenever he asked her to do something she really didn't want to do. He didn't think he would miss that face as much as he did the rest of the year.

"Nope, I don't see it." Natalie looked closer at the picture of the woman.

"You don't have it anymore. You don't have the nose either," he reminded her gently.

"I know," she whispered, and he almost missed it. The topic of the accident was not one that came easy for either of them, apparently.

"Did you read about her?" He squished a little closer to her, so they both could see the computer without moving it.

"Yes. She's married with two little kids. Lives in the town she grew up in. Has been a judge for around five years now. I got a letter from her once—must have been right before she became a judge. She was a lawyer and didn't say anything about having kids or being married. Maybe she would have said something if I had written her back. I didn't. She would have sent a picture too." Natalie scanned the write-up on her birth mother.

"Can I look at something?" He opened another window on the computer and started to search for something else.

"What?" She leaned closer to him.

"The husband's name is unique. Let's see if anything comes up." He hit enter on the screen. The top website was about a bed-and-breakfast in the town the judge was from and currently lived. "Look, it seems like her husband has a B&B. Okay, it says here that it's been open for around four years and is owned and operated by Max Valentine."

"No, it can't be true. Why would he have a B&B? She's a judge." She took the mouse under his hands that were resting on the keyboard and pulled up some pictures, clicking through them. In order to stay balanced, she was holding on to his arm with the hand not working the computer.

Without thinking about it, he lifted the arm that she was holding on to and put it around her body, pulling her close to him. All his senses were alive with her being so close—she was practically sitting on his lap. Her hand had moved and was resting on his upper thigh. If she moved her hand only two inches, she would be able to feel his rock-hard erection, something he couldn't control when she was so close and smelled so good.

Now all he saw was her hand wrapped around him with that sparkle in her green eyes. It didn't help things when she squeezed his thigh and turned to him with the eyes he was just imagining.

"Look, Sam." She took her hand off his thigh and pointed at the screen, but Sam was not able to concentrate on the screen anymore. "Look, the B&B is across from her law firm, Hart & Associates. It has to be her husband's."

"Should we go and stay there?" he asked, catching her excitement about the find.

"We?" She pulled away.

"I mean you; you should go stay there," he corrected quickly.

"I can't go alone. I'd be too nervous."

"Maybe a friend? Let's see if there are any openings." He hoped there were more.

Opening the reservations box, he saw that they had openings every day; no dates were blocked out. After clicking the date, he typed her name into the name box and then put in two guests.

"No," she stated quietly. "She'll know my name. At least the Natalie part. She named me," she whispered as she watched him type more.

"They kept the name she gave you?" He somehow managed to pull her even closer to him.

"Yes, they fell in love with it. They said it was perfect. Natalie means Christmas, and they thought I was the best Christmas present they ever got, even though I was not born at Christmas time. And my middle name is Hart, her last name. But Mom thought it was perfect. She liked to call me Natalie Hart before she died." She wiped away a tear from her eye.

"Okay, do you want to wait?" he asked.

"No, I want to be there on Thursday." She looked at her information on the reservation lines. Or maybe it was the two he had typed. "Can you come with me?"

"I don't know, Natalie. We barely know each other." He wanted to add he would never be able to keep his hands off her for days at a stretch.

Sitting up, she looked at him. "I don't have anyone to go with. It's my birthday on Thursday, and I want to see her on my birthday. It seems fitting. Please, Sam," she begged.

"Fine, you spoiled brat. I blame your dad for this." He pulled her back into his arms for a hug. Having her near him and in his arms seemed so natural.

"Let's change the reservation name to Sam and Beckett Sullivan. You used to yell at me a lot with my last name, so it should come naturally." Smiling, she moved his fingers off the keys and typed the words herself. She hit submit and wiggled beside him with excitement.

He centered the computer more on his lap, watching her do a little dance of excitement. Before he could stop her, she pushed the computer away and crawled on top of him , straddling his legs. The giggles couldn't be contained when she hugged him and said, "Thank you, thank you."

Her entire body was wiggling on his, and he had to grit his teeth to suppress a moan at the feeling. Quickly, he grabbed her hips to stop her from sliding up his lap and over his erection. That move would be too much for him to take.

Since she was so tall, she was looking down at him from her spot on his lap. Taking his face in her hands, she said, "Are you ready to be married to me?"

Then, to his surprise, she lowered her lips to his and kissed him lightly. Just a whisper of a touch with her warm breath washing over his skin. As soon as he registered what was happening, it was over. She pulled away with a grin.

Before he could pull her back to him, she rolled off his lap and practically jumped off the bed. Heading for the door, she called out, "I have to go talk to my dad. Hope he has clothes on by now!"

Listening to her laughter as she walked down the hallway away from him, he let out the groan he had been suppressing. Had he just agreed to play her husband for three days? Had he just let her kiss him? Had he just almost slid her up so that her heat would be resting on his erection?

When was he going to learn to control himself when she was around? He hoped he could pull himself together by the time she came back from her dad's house. Getting up, he needed a cold shower, and he had better get used to them. It was going to be a long few days.

CHAPTER 5

Slamming out of Sam's back door, Natalie was practically dancing with excitement. Her dad had a girlfriend, she was going to see her mother, and Sam was packing heat. Though she hadn't really tried to notice, it was hard not to when it was right there between them. If she wasn't so excited about their trip, she might have pointed it out to see if he would blush.

He was still really fun to tease.

Rushing across the two lawns, she nearly screamed when someone stood up from the patio chair on her dad's deck. She put her hand on her heart and breathed heavily, trying to catch her breath.

"So, you have been hiding across the yard? That one I did not see coming," Mia said as she sat back down in the chair. No longer in pink, but in jeans and an orange T-shirt that had seen better days. It went along with what Natalie could only assume was a massive hangover, based on the sunglasses and pale complexion.

"Mia, you scared the daylights out of me," Natalie said when she could finally catch her breath. Natalie took the chair across from her and sat down. Taking in the half-empty bottle of water and empty bag of chips, she wondered how long Mia had been waiting for her.

"What about me when my Jeep was still in the parking lot?" Mia slid off her sunglasses, tossing them on the table and then squinting in the sunlight.

"Sorry, Sam caught me and brought me to his house." She had texted Mia she was okay, but she had forgotten about the Jeep she was supposed to take.

"Sam, is it?" Mia raised her eyebrow in question.

"It's not like that. You have a dirty mind, Mia."

"Hey, you were the one who practically danced over here. Looks like a post-sex dance to me," Mia replied, though her one eye was squinting when she smiled.

"No sex. I was supposed to get married yesterday," Natalie reminded her, though she shouldn't have to.

"But you didn't," Mia pointed out.

"Thanks to you. You didn't have to let me go." Natalie was nothing but happy about the turn of events. All worry and concern gone.

"You were not making it down that aisle. You knew it wasn't right."

"You're right. I don't love him. After seeing Tess and Ruth with their guys, I knew I didn't have that with Jason. Nothing even close to that."

"I knew you had to leave when you were starting to babble about Henry. You're not ready to get married if you're still hung up on your first love," Mia explained.

Natalie leaned back into her chair and looked at her friend, ignoring the comment completely. "Did you go to the reception?"

"No, I stayed to clean the church, and then it was late. I went home." She looked up at the cloudless sky, not meeting her eyes.

"But Dad had the reception, didn't he?" Natalie wanted to make sure.

"Yes, you'll have to ask him about it. I did hear that Jason was making out with one of the bridesmaids, who I thought were all his sisters." Mia was excited about the gossip despite the hangover.

"One was my college friend," Natalie informed her.

"So, we are two-thirds sure that it was his sister," Mia decided with a giggle and a groan of pain. "And odds are that it was his sister."

"Is my dad home?" Natalie changed the subject from Jason and what might have happened after she left.

"He's gone right now. Church." Mia pointed out the obvious. Her dad did not miss church.

"I forgot," Natalie admitted.

"So, the happiness is not about sex. Close to sex?" she asked with a grin.

"No, nothing like that. It's Mr. Sullivan." Though she had stopped seeing him as just a teacher hours ago, around the time she fell asleep in his arms.

"How has Mr. Sullivan put that smile on your face?" Mia inquired.

"He's going with me to see my mom." Natalie put it out there. As she had told Sam, nobody knew she was adopted.

Mia's mouth opened in a shocked expression, and she breathed out, "But she's dead. Isn't she?"

"Yes, Lara Beckett is dead. But I was adopted, and we're going to see my birth mother. Just to see, not meet or anything," Natalie explained, hating that she didn't feel like she was betraying the mom who raised her.

"Why didn't I know you were adopted?" Mia demanded as if the entire world knew but her. That she was the last to find out. The big secret kept from her.

"Because nobody knew. And I still don't want anyone to know. Patrick and Lara are my parents," Natalie stated firmly. Mia was the biggest gossip in town, so she had to be told when things were not for everyone to know.

"Okay. When are you going?" she asked.

"Today. I think I need to get away for a little bit. I can't hole up at Sam's for the week," Natalie stated.

"I could. He's quite sexy," Mia purred.

"Mia, really?" Natalie laughed, hating how she hated Mia saying it.

"Oh, yeah. Sexy Sam," Mia said.

"I should hook you guys up when we get back. He is really nice." But the words stuck in her throat. She loved Mia and wanted her to be happy, but could she just hand over Sam to her? She had no claim to the man, but it seemed that her heart thought she did.

"No, thank you. Sexy Sam is going to be here forever. I'm getting out of here soon." Mia had always said she was moving before she turned thirty, but that was next year, and she seemed to be wavering on her plan.

"Here I thought I could find you and get the girls together, and we could do something for a few days. But no, you have something planned already," Mia said about the book club.

Natalie looked at her friend—that would have been amazing. A week of fun with her new friends. Maybe she should cancel the mom thing and do that. *No*, she thought, *this is my birthday week, and I need to go. Doing anything else would just be chickening out.*

"That would have been so much fun," Natalie agreed.

"Nothing like meeting the woman who gave you life." Mia smiled at her.

"I never wanted to meet her, then last week, bam! I wanted her at my wedding. Like she needed to be there for some reason. Just like Hazel, I needed her there for no reason, just a feeling." Natalie tried to explain her feelings, but it didn't sound right.

"I don't know. Maybe it was someone telling you that marrying him wasn't right for you. I mean, you have a ton of guardian angels. Your mom, Hanna and Henry, maybe Jamie. A lot of people up there are watching you. Just remember that when you get down and dirty with Sam. A lot of eyes watching," Mia said with a wink and a laugh.

Natalie looked at Mia seriously, ignoring the last part. "Do you really think my mom wanted my birth mom there, and the twins wanted Hazel there? Maybe so they can see her? Do you think they're watching out for Hazel too?"

"I hope so. Hazel needs more watching than you do." Mia leaned back in her chair and looked at the sky, immediately closing her eyes against the bright light.

"That's another thing that kept bothering me, my talk with Hazel last week. I wanted to ask her if she wanted to learn to do the podcasting stuff when I was gone. But she flipped out. She told me that we weren't friends when we were young, that I was friends with Hanna but not with her. She was just the third wheel. Looking back on those days, she was right. I hung out with her only because she was Hanna's sister. I wasn't a good friend to her. It made me sad to think I was a mean person. I hate to see her hurting now, but maybe I hurt her before the accident too." Natalie didn't want to cry again, but she felt a tear leave her eye.

"It sounds like meeting up with Hazel again has dug up some emotions you thought you were over. Survivor's guilt that wasn't dealt with. I've heard both you and Hazel apologize for surviving the accident, except both of you are lucky to have survived. You two have to get past the emotions of surviving. You should think about that this week while you're gone."

"I have a lot to think about this week," Natalie agreed as they heard the sliding door open behind them. Patrick stuck his head out in concern, and Mia excused herself and left, leaving the father and daughter alone.

Natalie had left him holding the bag yesterday, but Patrick didn't seem bothered by it. He looked the same as always: a short, balding middle-aged man. But he was her dad, and she loved him. Over the years, she had tried to not disappoint him, but yesterday had to be bad.

"Sorry, Dad," was all she could think to say as she watched him sit in the chair Mia had abandoned.

"Nothing to be sorry about, Natalie. It's better that you realized it yesterday than marry a man you didn't love. There's nothing worse than marrying a man you don't love. You made a lot of people talk, but then so did he after you left. It will all die down in a few days."

"I thought I loved him. Now I'm sure I never did. I loved the idea of him, of someone like him," she admitted, happy she wasn't on her honeymoon when the realization hit. When it was too late.

"One day, you will meet someone, and you will know the difference. Love is a powerful thing." Her dad leaned toward her, a sadness in his eyes.

"Do you still love Mom?" She needed to know if their love had survived without the woman.

"Yes, I love that she gave me you. I love the life we had. I will love her for the rest of my life." He leaned back in his chair.

"Do you love Faith?" She had to ask, to see if he would admit it. Or if he would lie about the relationship.

He raised an eyebrow and chucked. "Yes, I have for a long time."

"Why didn't you tell me?"

"You weren't ready when we started seeing each other. I don't know if you remember, but you were very opinionated in high school. Then the accident, and that took years to get over. By that time, Faith and I had settled into a pattern. Her kids were getting older, and they didn't want a dad," Patrick rambled.

"How old are her kids?"

"Ten, eleven, and thirteen. All boys." He shrugged.

"I think it's time for you to take the next step with her. You should ask her to move in with you or you move in with her. You deserve happiness, Dad, and they would be getting a great dad." Natalie leaned forward and took her dad's hands in hers. "If you need a reference, I will give you a great one."

"I don't know." Patrick squeezed his hand.

"Just talk to her. I'm going to move out. Ruth has to have a place I can rent. I should let you have your time."

"I don't want you moving out."

She shook her head at him. "I don't want to live with a bunch of rowdy kids, but you do."

"I don't," he argued, but he was smiling. He was great with kids, and those kids would be lucky to have him in their lives.

"Of course you do, and maybe you could have a few of your own. I could have a baby sister." Natalie watched her dad's eyes light up a little at the thought.

"I don't think that will be happening," he informed her with a grin.

"If I remember correctly, she just had her fortieth birthday last month. Still young." She wanted her dad to have a family and love big enough that she would stop feeling guilty.

"Maybe you will have babies soon," came his hopeful response.

Natalie dropped his hand and leaned back. "The doctors don't think so. Too much damage."

"No, they said that it would be a high-risk pregnancy, not that it wouldn't happen, Natalie Hart." He always used her mom's nickname when he was trying to make a point. He had been in on her appointments, embarrassingly almost all of them. He knew it all, even something as personal as her reproductive system.

"A lot happened down there, Dad. I don't want you to get your hopes very high." Or hers, for that matter.

"My hopes are always high for you." He leaned back in his chair with a smile on his face.

"Are you mad about Sam?" she questioned him.

"What about him? That he took you home?" Her dad looked at her.

"That I stayed at his place last night." Not saying that she had slept with him on his couch for most of it.

"No, I know Sam. He's a decent guy. Did something happen?" He sat up straight, and a flash of worry crossed his face.

"No, he was great. He saved me when I needed him the most." Even to her, it sounded dramatic.

"Again." Patrick smiled at her and rubbed her leg.

"What do you mean, again?" she questioned.

"He did chest compressions on you after the accident until the ambulance came. He saved your life that day," her dad explained.

"I didn't know." It was the truth; she had never heard much about that night. Nobody wanted to talk about what had happened after the crash. Mostly her.

"You weren't conscious then, or for months afterward."

"I will have to thank him." She remembered the sadness in his eyes when she talked about Hanna and Henry.

"I have many times," Patrick confessed.

Biting her lip, she took a deep breath and said, "Sam is taking me to see my mom today. I'm not replacing you and Mom; I just want to meet her, see what she's like."

"I knew one day you would want to. You just needed something to push you in that direction. You're taking Sam?"

"I don't want to go alone, and he's so nice. I hope you don't mind."

"Nothing for me to mind, Natalie. If something happens between you two, I will not be upset. I actually think you two have a lot in common." His words shook her. During the two years of her relationship with Jason, he was indifferent to it the entire time. But for some reason, he seemed happy if anything happened with Sam.

"But you know that if something happens this week, I'm going to wait at least eight years to tell you about it. In payback." She laughed as he joined in when he made the connection.

"When you get back, we'll all have dinner. I can properly introduce you to Faith and the boys, and you can bring Sam if you want to. If something happens."

"That'll be great. I want you to be happy, Dad. If she makes you happy, I'm okay with anything you decide." She fought back tears of happiness.

"Right back at you, kid." He tapped her leg.

"I have to get some stuff for my trip." She gave her dad a hug and went into her bedroom. As she picked out some more clothes she would need for the trip, she thought about her dad's reaction to her and Sam being more than friends. Would he really be okay with her dating one of his friends?

When she had her stuff together, she headed back to Sam's, but when she got to the patio, her dad was still sitting in the chair she left him in. His face was sad as he looked at the green grass in the yard.

Sitting down again, she asked, "Are you okay?"

He turned to her. "Yeah, I'm okay. Yesterday I thought I was giving you away, but now I'm giving you away today."

"You'll have me forever," Natalie said.

"No, after today I will share you with her. Giving you to a husband was easier than giving you back to her. Here's the movie I made. It doesn't include any wedding stuff as I haven't had time to work on it lately." He placed a disk in her hand. Natalie looked at the disk that contained her life—nobody's life was as documented as her life had been.

Hugging her dad as they both cried in the backyard, she wondered if he was right, and their relationship would forever change after today. But she knew it would change, especially if he and Faith moved on with their relationship. Was it possible that they had already spent the last night under the same roof? Eating a quiet meal together? That they hadn't even noticed that it had happened? She didn't want what they had for so many years to change but knew it already had.

With everything she had, she pulled out of his arms and headed across the yard to Sam's house. The walk was short, but at the property line, she turned around, and he waved at her. Smiling at him, she turned and went through back door and into her future.

CHAPTER 6

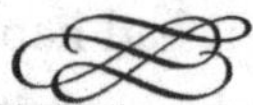

Natalie and Sam didn't leave Landstad until after lunch. It had taken them longer than expected to get their stuff packed and Sam to get his house ready to be gone for almost a week. They were going to take his truck but then realized it was still wet on the inside from the day before. So, Natalie had gone home to get her SUV. Now they had loaded it and were finally off.

They chatted easily as the flat countryside rolled by, neither taking much notice of the green fields surrounding them. That was what North Dakota looked like in the summer: flat and green, and they were both used to it. After two hours, they crossed into Minnesota, but the landscape didn't change much for a while.

"We're going to get there late, aren't we?" Natalie looked out the window as farmland started to turn to small lakes and swamps.

When she had made it back from her dad's, she had been in tears, but not the gut-wrenching tears of the previous day. Though she hadn't shared what she and her dad had talked about, Sam could tell she was more at peace about the almost wedding.

"No, I changed the reservation a little after you left this morning. I said we would be there from Tuesday to Saturday." He hoped she wouldn't be mad at him for not talking to her about it first. After all, it was her trip, not his.

"What are we going to do until then?" Her green eyes bored into his.

He turned away from the road. "My parents have a cabin in Brainerd. I thought we could stay there. Have a few days between the wedding and the meeting."

"On a lake?" was all she asked.

"Yes."

"Why do they have a cabin so far away? We've been driving forever." She looked out the window again.

"Because they live in Fargo, and it's only half the distance we're going to travel." The distance had made it hard for him to go to the cabin often. Although he made it there at least once a summer, he would love to do so more often.

"I never thought of you being from anywhere. Are you from Fargo then?" She sounded amazed.

"Born and raised."

"Do you want to go back there?" Her green eyes stared at him with interest as she shifted in her seat.

"No, not in years. I like my job and the town. I like the small school." It was true. Except for the year of the accident, he had never thought about looking for a job elsewhere.

"But you're not married or anything?"

"Nope, the dating pool is small. The one drawback of a small town."

"What about Mia?" she asked.

"Mia at the diner?" He had known the woman for years, but there had never been anything between them. In fact, he hadn't seen her as a possible person to date since they didn't run in the same circles. Mostly he assumed she was already dating someone.

"Yes, she's your age and a lot of fun."

"I guess I've never noticed her like that before," he admitted, and the car fell into silence as he drove through the countryside. Glancing over, he saw her looking out the window, but every now and then, she would shift in her seat.

"Do you want to stop?" he asked as she slid her hand behind her back and winced.

"How far is it?"

"About an hour still." He was familiar enough with this drive after all these years.

"Could we? I can't sit that much longer. My back starts to hurt."

He pulled over in the next town they came to. "What do you want to do?"

"Can we just walk? It helps." She opened the door and stiffly got out.

Sam jumped out, circled the car, and took her hand as they started to walk down the sidewalk. Should he let go of her hand? Why had he grabbed it? They were only friends, and he should drop it. But she was holding on as tightly as he was, so he held on. "How bad is your back?"

"Getting better. It hurts when I don't get to move enough, like in the car," she admitted.

"From the accident?" he questioned, even though he already knew. She had been perfect and athletic before that happened.

"Yes, it was broken in two places. But I was lucky, and they were able to fuse it back together. I wasn't paralyzed. A little back pain is fine compared to not feeling my body anymore." She laughed at her own pain.

"How about we don't talk about the accident? Do you still play sports?" He tried to change the subject. She had been a three-sport athlete: volleyball, basketball, and track. Despite her height, she had been agile and graceful enough to be good at anything she tried. She had even had scholarships from a college that she lost because of the accident. If it hadn't happened, he wondered what she would have achieved.

"No," was all she said, not elaborating as they walked.

"No, that's it?" he questioned teasingly.

"Not since the accident. See? Not so easy not to talk about it," she said sadly.

"I guess it isn't something that you can put in the back of your mind."

"No, it's always there. Something always reminds me." Lifting the arm he held, she pulled up the sleeve on her T-shirt that came to her elbow. Once the sleeve was up two inches, there was an angry red line just over an inch long and jagged and rough. "My bone went through the skin about an inch. They set it and sewed me up that first night. But they were fixing and sewing so much that they weren't taking their time with the stitches, so many of them healed with the stitches visible. They can fix it, but it involves cutting them back open and stitching them back up. A lot of pointless pain. I stopped the surgeries like that a few years ago. I was tired of being in pain. I have a lot of scars like this, some better, some worse."

Taking her arm gently in his hands, he ran a finger over the scar; it felt as jagged as it looked. "Why didn't they take more time that first night?"

"I wasn't expected to make it. Less than a 25 percent chance that first day. No need for great stitches to put me in the ground." She was looking down at her arm where he held it, stroking it with his fingers.

His attention was trapped on the puckered scar—it was the only blemish on her smooth olive skin. Without thinking, he lowered his lips and gently kissed the evidence of her survival, of what she had endured.

His lips touched the warm skin, and he heard her gasp. Slowing, he raised his head to look at her shocked face. Her green eyes held his, but she wasn't upset or angry at what he had done; instead, her eyes showed surprise and something he couldn't describe. Dropping her arm, he carefully took her jaw in his hands and brushed his lips across her cheek, murmuring, "The scars mean you're alive. They only heal when you survive what you have endured."

Her newly freed hands ran up his chest to rest on his beating heart. Gently, he rained kisses across her cheeks and her nose. His mouth was moving toward hers when a car honked nearby, causing them to both jump away from each other.

Once apart, Sam didn't dare look over at Natalie because he knew he had gone too far. It seemed one touch would lead to another and another. Though she took his hand in hers to walk back to the car, neither spoke. Was she thinking about what would have happened if they had kissed? He was.

Back on the road, the conversation turned to the landscapes and the passing cars. He cursed himself for almost kissing her. What was he thinking? She almost got married yesterday. But only almost.

She finally looked over at him and asked, "What do your parents do?"

"My dad is a teacher also, and Mom stayed at home with us kids."

"How many kids?" she asked in surprise.

"Three. My two brothers work together in real estate. Both are married with kids," he told her.

"Where are you? Oldest? Youngest? What are their names?" She turned her body toward him.

"I'm the baby. They're Seth and Steven," he said with a smile.

"Your mom had a theme. I like that."

Did she wish she had siblings? "Are you going to have a theme when you have kids?" he asked, wondering if his mom actually had a theme or just ended up with a theme.

"No, I'm not having kids." Her voice went flat as she turned to look out the passenger window.

Reaching over, he took her hand in his. "You would be a great mom. You could teach them all your basketball moves."

She laughed at his words and squeezed his hand. "It's not that I don't want them, Sam. I want to adopt one day."

"The accident?" he asked, knowing her decision was based on that day. Most of her life either stopped or started on that day.

"Yes, too much internal stuff. I won't go into the gory details, but it is close to impossible for me to get pregnant or stay that way. I have had to accept it, and I do. When I find that someone, I plan to start the adoption process right away." He could tell by her answer that though she was sad at giving up her dream of not having her own kids, she was excited about raising a baby that needed a family, like her parents had.

Turning off the main road, he drove through the weaving road the led to his parent's cabin. When he had called his mom this morning, they had been here, but she said they were leaving to go home today. As the trees gave way to the house, he saw that their car was still there. Of course, his mom wouldn't leave if she knew he was bringing a woman here, even though he had explained they were just friends. That they were in no way dating.

"This is it. And my parents are *still* here." He tried not to sound annoyed but knew he had failed.

She was looking out the windshield at his parents' dream house and said, "I was envisioning something smaller. Wow, this is nice."

The older couple had saved for years to afford the cabin, so it was big enough to host the entire family without it feeling crowded. In the daytime, it also had amazing views of the lake from floor-to-ceiling windows and decks.

"I know. They bought it about ten years ago." Stopping the car, he got out and grabbed their suitcases out of the back end.

Just as Natalie was getting out stiffly—he could tell her back was bothering her again—his parents walked out the front door. He could tell just by looking at them that they were planning the wedding as he and Natalie had been driving here. They had been waiting for him to find someone, and they would latch on to anyone he brought around.

"Mom and Dad, this is Natalie Beckett. Natalie, these are my parents, Sue and Steve Sullivan." He watched them shake hands, and then his mother gave Natalie a hug. Like a woman desperate for another daughter-in-law.

"I'm so glad Sammy brought you to visit us." His mother, who was considered tall for a woman, was still a few inches shorter than Natalie. The older woman kept her arm around Natalie as she ushered her into the house. Not letting her go, as if when she did, the woman would disappear.

Steve watched them go, and when Sam got close enough, he said, "She's exactly what you need, son."

"Dad, you barely know her. And she almost got married yesterday," he reminded him. His parents were not interested in facts, it seemed. Just a warm-blooded woman for him.

"Almost, Sam, almost. She didn't get away." Steve chuckled and slapped him on the back as they entered the cabin.

Sam took the suitcases to two of the spare rooms upstairs and went back down to save Natalie from his parents. Maybe he hadn't brought home a woman in years, but was that any reason to smother the one he did bring home? If anything, it would make him not want to ever bring home anyone else.

Seeing Natalie chatting with his parents as if they hadn't just met was going to be enough to question anyone else he might bring. Not that he had ever been close to bringing a woman here.

"Sammy, I'm heating you and Natalie some supper. You sit with her and explain some of the pictures. She probably doesn't know what your brothers look like." His mom was busy in the kitchen.

Sitting down next to Natalie, he saw she was flipping through the photo album. It was something Sam wouldn't have even guessed was at the cabin. There were dozens of them at the house he had been raised in, and it seemed there were a few here. Just his luck.

Looking up, her eyes were sparkling with excitement. "You need to bring more girls home, Sammy."

He cringed at the nickname he had long outgrown. "I didn't think it would be this bad."

Watching her as she went back to looking at pictures, he wished for a moment that it was real, that she was his. But he knew that wouldn't happen. She was, after all, his former student.

Turning, she looked at him with a smile as she pointed to one. "This is you?"

Looking at the picture of a little boy in only shorts holding up a fish almost as big as he was, he said, "Yes, I was four, I think."

"You haven't changed at all. Still blonde and so sure of yourself." She looked up from the picture, and their eyes caught.

"I am not," he argued but couldn't not smile at her.

Reaching out, she touched his hair. "Yes, you are."

"I'm not sure of myself," he insisted.

"Since the first day I met you. Why do you think I had to come up with a nickname? It was to bring you down a notch," she whispered, pretending to analyze another picture.

"You said Hanna did that." He squinted at her.

"Hanna, me … Same thing in those days." She pointed at people in the pictures, and he gave their names and how they were related if needed. Even the backstory on the photo if he knew it. Some stories were embellished a bit to make her laugh—he had always liked her laugh.

Looking up at one point, he saw his parents watching them, both grinning. Before long, his mother brought the soup and sandwiches to the table, and Natalie closed the photo album and put it aside.

As the younger couple ate, the older couple watched and talked.

"How long have you known Sam?" his dad asked Natalie.

"Six years, I suppose, but I've been away from town for many of them." Natalie took a big bite from her sandwich, probably hoping his parents would stop with the questions. Sam knew it wouldn't work. These two were tenacious.

"Were you his student? You look young enough." His mom said it as a compliment, but it was more of her looking for information.

"Thank you, Mrs. Sullivan. I don't feel young some days. Yes," she admitted with a nod, "he started my senior year."

"She made my life miserable," Sam interjected, hoping his parents would stop seeing them as a couple, because they were not.

"I have apologized for that." Natalie shot him a smile.

"All I remember from your first year teaching, Sam, was that it was bad. I don't remember much about why." His mom scrunched up her face as she tried to remember.

Sam glared at her, hoping she would get the hint and would stop talking about it.

"Wasn't that the year you were going to quit? Around Christmas time? It had to be, because you had just started there," Steve asked Sam, all interested in the timeline.

"Yes," he said through clenched teeth, but he didn't think his parents were catching on.

"Was I that bad?" Natalie chuckled and stopped eating, looking over at him with those big green eyes.

"No, dear," his mother assured her. "There was a bad car accident that he worked on that really got to him. It took months for him to get over it. Or maybe he just got better at covering it up. He stopped talking about it."

"Oh," was all Natalie said. Putting her spoon down, she got up and silently went to the bathroom off the kitchen. Her movements were stiff and shaky, and Sam wanted to follow her, to explain everything.

"Did I say something?" his mother asked innocently, her eyes also watching Natalie leave the room.

"She was in that accident, Mom. She's the only one who survived," he said as low as possible, though Natalie was well aware of what happened during the accident.

"Well, you could have said," his mother defended herself.

"I didn't want to. The accident has so much to do with her past, I don't want it to define her now." He wanted his parents to like her for who she was, not because she had an accident once. One that she couldn't seem to get over.

"I like her, Sam," his mom proclaimed. "You can't let her get away. You need to marry her."

"Marriage, Mom? You met her less than an hour ago, and we are not dating," he reminded her, but he was sure she didn't care.

"I'm with your mom. This one's a keeper," his dad added.

Before he could protest more, Natalie came out of the bathroom. He could tell she had been crying again. Without coming to the table, she walked to the stairway. "Is my room up here? I think I'm going to just go to bed; it was a long trip. Thank you for supper, Mrs. Sullivan. It was delicious."

"Yes, just pick a room. I didn't ask Sam if you wanted one or two," his mom sang out and hurried over to Natalie. "If you want to share with him, it's okay. We are very progressive around here."

Sam watched them walk up the stairs in disbelief. Never had his mother let her sons share a room with their girlfriends—not until they were married. His mother really wanted him married. Taking another bite of the sandwich, he wondered if she would talk Natalie into sharing a bedroom with him.

He looked across the table at his dad, who was watching them going up the stairs with a big grin on his face. Would they have him and Natalie engaged before they left for Birch Cove in two days?

CHAPTER 7

NATALIE LET the cold air make her shiver as she leaned against the deck railing. In the summer, she loved the feeling of being cold. In the winter, she loved being warm, sitting by a fire, or snuggled in a blanket. But in the summer, she loved to go out in the dark and just let the cold air surround her and cool her from the outside.

"Are you cold?" Sam's voice came from behind, startling her.

When had he come out?

After going upstairs with his mom, she hadn't left her room. Though she hadn't thought she was tired, she had instantly fallen asleep when she laid down. Her back had woken her nearly an hour ago, and after taking a pain pill, she had sat in bed reading until she couldn't sit there anymore. She needed to move.

Coming down to the main floor to stand on the deck and look out into the dark night was what she had needed, so here she was. But she wasn't alone anymore. How was she supposed to get him out of her mind if he was always there?

"No," she answered. "Just needed to cool down."

Turning, she saw he was in a deck chair by the patio table. He was just wearing basketball shorts, no shirt, no shoes. Walking over to the chair next to him, she sat down and curled her legs under her.

"Couldn't sleep?" He looked her over. She was wearing a tank top and short shorts for the warm night.

"My back woke me."

"Does it wake you every night?"

"No, I have exercises that I'm supposed to do to help, but with the wedding and everything, I haven't been doing them."

"Maybe you need to start them again, so you can sleep all night."

Even though it was dark, there was enough moonlight for her to see his smile. She liked his smile. "Why are you up?"

"Nightmare," was all he said.

Taking a deep breath, she guessed, "About the accident?"

"Yes. I still get them every now and then. Stress, usually, but we've been talking about it a lot these last few days." He ran his fingers through his sleep-tussled hair.

"I'm glad I have no memories or dreams of that night." It was a small gift.

"What's the last thing you remember?"

Closing her eyes, she leaned her head back on the chair. "We were heading home and had been drinking at the party. We were all buzzed. I remember Hanna and Jamie were making out in the back seat, but Henry and I were fighting. He was taking me home. We had broken up at the party. I never told anyone that. He wanted more, and I wasn't ready. I should have. I think about that now. Would sex be different before and after the accident? I don't know. Anyway, he started to yell at me a little about it, without Hanna and Jamie knowing what we were talking about. Then he lost control, and I hit my head on something right away. I don't remember anything."

"I remember everything. So much blood, so many bodies. You were lucky you landed in Grace and Ken's place. Grace saved you. The rest were already dead, but Grace worked on you until the helicopter came. She kept you breathing." She could tell by his voice he had turned in his chair toward her.

Her eyes were shut still. "I'm sorry you still have nightmares because of me," she whispered.

"I'm just glad you're alive. I didn't think you would survive the trip to the hospital." His voice was hoarse.

Opening her eyes, she looked at him, but his brown eyes were already on her.

"How did you know it was me? I saw the video Dad took after I came out of surgery that night. My face was …" She didn't finish.

He pulled her onto his lap, and she went willingly, needing his warmth, his strength. His arms went around her, and she laid her head on his shoulder.

"Your jacket. You had on Henry's jacket like always. And the hair, I knew your hair." He touched the curly strands flowing over her shoulder. "My world came crashing down that night. I was in shock for a few days after. I couldn't believe God would take you all away in one moment."

"I'm glad I wasn't conscious for months. When I did wake up, I think my brain was still scrambled because I couldn't comprehend for a while that they were gone. That nothing was going to be the same again." She rested her hands on his bare chest, feeling his steady heartbeat. Feeling safe, even as they talked about the worst day of her life.

His body radiated enough heat that Natalie couldn't feel the chilly air around her. Noticing that the darkness was not as dark anymore, she felt Sam turn the chair so she could see the sun starting to rise over the lake. The previous day, she hadn't noticed the large body of water on this side of the cabin, but it was beautiful in the first rays of sunshine. Even better when she was in Sam's arms.

"Did you bring a swimsuit?" His eyes didn't leave the sunrise.

"No, I wasn't told about the stop at the cabin." Reminding him, she ran her hand up to his shoulder, loving the feel of his solid muscles under her hand.

"I'll see what Mom can scrounge up. Dad bought a new boat this year." His arms were still tight around her.

"A boat ride would be fun." Smiling, her head rested on his shoulder.

As the sun's warm rays chased off the shadows of the night, Natalie knew she had to go. It didn't matter how nice it had been to be on his lap, in his arms. Soon, her scars would be very visible with her only in a tank top and short shorts. Right now, she didn't want him to have the reminders of that night so visible.

Trying to be as graceful as possible, she pushed herself away from his shoulder and got to her feet. But she accidentally tripped over his feet, and if he hadn't grabbed her, she would've landed on her butt. Hiding her embarrassment behind a laugh she said, "Sorry."

"That's okay." He stood up with more grace.

"I should go," she mumbled as her hand went automatically to her chest to cover scars the tank top left visible.

"Natalie." His words stopped her, and she looked at him. "Be proud of the scars. They say that you're a survivor."

"Easy for you to say, Sam, you don't have to wear them for the rest of your life." Turning, she went into the house to get ready for the day ahead. One that might include swimming and a new boat.

CHAPTER 8

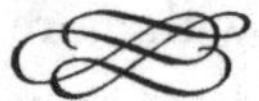

Sam was determined to spend the rest of the day without talking about the accident. Natalie was emotionally rung out and needed to relax. She had been through a lot over the past few days, and she couldn't take much more. From the wedding to talking about lost loved ones, she needed some time to just be herself again. He was determined to give her a day of fun.

The afternoon sun was high above their heads as they floated in the middle of the lake alone on his dad's boat. Sam had shut the engine down, and they were just letting the current take them where it wanted to go. Natalie was wearing the swimming suit that his mom had found earlier; though it wasn't an exact fit, it was the closest she had after putting it on. But so far, Sam had not seen it, she had worn an oversized T-shirt all day. Not that Natalie Beckett in an oversized T-shirt that hit her at mid-thigh wasn't hot in itself, especially because it showed off her long legs. Scars and all.

Sam had taken off his shirt the moment they had left shore and was just wearing his swim trunks, letting the hot sun beat down on him. But Natalie was all covered up. He was not going to make her take off the shirt if she didn't want to. Not today.

"Are you mad about your dad and Faith? I didn't actually know you didn't know." Sam was sitting in one of the lounge chairs in the front of the boat, trying not to steal glances at Natalie, who was sitting across from him, her eyes closed against the bright sun.

"No, I was happy for him," she admitted.

"Is he going to take it into the open now?" he asked.

"I think so. I told him to marry her." Her eyes didn't open as she spoke.

"Do you think he will?" Sam was surprised Natalie would be ready for her dad to marry already. Since she hadn't even known the man was dating.

"I think so. He says he loves her. I know he wants to help raise her kids." The sunlight was bouncing off her black hair.

"Yeah, he likes the kids."

"I told him they should have some of their own. I wouldn't mind." Still, her eyes didn't open, but she smiled at her announcement.

"I think he will have a lot of work in front of him convincing her to start over with a baby." After knowing them for years, he didn't think Faith wanted more kids. Three boys alone were a lot to handle. And no matter how much work Natalie had been as a teen, Faith's boys were going to be worse.

"We're going to get together so I can meet her when I get back. I mean, I know her, but not as Dad's girlfriend. That's different," she said behind her closed lids.

"Do you think you'll like her as his girlfriend?" He still watched her, mostly because he couldn't look away.

She shook her head at him. "I already like her. I just want her to know that I like her with my dad. That I'm not some kid who doesn't want her parent happy."

Smiling, he asked, "Can you swim?"

"Yes, I can even save your life if I need to. Or if I want to." Sitting up, she laughed at his pained expression.

He loved when he could get her to laugh. Watching her stand up and walk to the back of the boat, he started to follow. As she walked, she pulled off the shirt, revealing the teal swimsuit underneath. Dropping the shirt, she climbed onto the diving platform on the back of the boat and spun in a circle before diving into the water below. It was so quick he hadn't even noticed any of her scars, just the perfect dive. As with anything sporty, Natalie could do it.

Hurrying, he climbed onto the diving platform himself and looked for her to surface. Panic rose up in him when she didn't immediately come up. He knew the water was deep enough for her dive, but he still worried, searching the deep, clear water for any signs of her. He was so focused on finding her at the bottom of the lake that when she pulled his legs out from under him, he wasn't ready and fell hard into the water below.

He was coughing when he surfaced, but she just laughed at him. Going after her, he realized that she was as agile in the water as outside of it, and he was unable to catch her. With that knowledge, he stopped and treaded water, waiting for her to come back to him. Like a fish, she would come back to the bait. She couldn't resist.

Her head disappeared under the water again, and he couldn't see her but knew she was coming for him. Laughing, he rolled in the water as she grabbed at his swimming trunks, trying to pull them off. Trying to catch her, he was unsuccessful again, and she darted away.

Before he could get himself back to treading water and looking for her, she bobbed out of the water, inches from his face. He watched her take a deep breath before she pushed him under. With her hands on his shoulders, she used all her force to push him as far under as she could and then slid her arms around his and went still.

Under the water, he opened his eyes and looked into her green ones as she held him suspended. His lungs were starting to burn with the need to breathe—he hadn't gotten a good breath in before she plunged him underwater. Blowing out the last of his air, he thought that she would let go. Feeling her laugh, she didn't let go of him but instead pulled him to the surface with a few quick kicks.

When they made it, he breathed the fresh air deeply—and then coughed once he was able to breathe again.

"I decided to save you, sexy Sam. Now I only owe you one more saving." She wiped the water from her face.

"I don't think it counts when you were the one trying to kill me,

Beckett," he grumped, using her last name like he used to when she was in school.

"I wasn't trying to kill you. You were supposed to have taken a bigger breath than you did. Not my fault." She was treading water not far from when he was, but at a bigger distance than before.

"Completely your fault," he mumbled, still mad as he swam past her to the boat.

Her recklessness had bothered him. It had reminded him of the girl she had been before the accident. It reminded him that she could be impulsive and thoughtless. It had reminded him that she was still a kid, still his student.

Climbing back on the boat, he sat in the captain's chair by the steering controls with a huff. The water had been cold, but the warm sun was taking the chill off his skin. Waiting for her to get back on the boat, he worked at getting control of his anger. This was her day to have fun; she didn't need his emotions getting in the way. But she had put them both in danger.

Sliding on his sunglasses, he watched as she climbed up the ladder and out of the water. Her face appeared looking cautious, a little nervous about seeing him. Was it because of how he had acted or that she wasn't wearing her T-shirt anymore? He watched as she set her resolve to not let whichever one it was bother her. As she came farther into view, he realized that her swimming suit was a size to small, barely containing her round breasts.

Ignoring him, she didn't look at him from the time she got on the boat, slid her discarded T-shirt back on, and returned to the chair she had been sitting in before they went swimming. Sitting with her arms around her knees, she stared off at the shoreline, silent.

He stomped over and plopped down angrily across from her. "Don't be like this, Natalie."

"Like what?" She didn't turn to look at him.

"Sad. We were having fun before you took it too far."

"I know. I'm sorry I acted like that. I was really having fun. I wasn't trying to hurt you. I sometimes just let her out, and I know I shouldn't. Things don't turn out right when I do. Things happen, people get hurt." She was still looking at the shoreline.

"Who is she?"

"The person I used to be before. The one that caused everyone so much trouble all the time. I really do try not to be her anymore," she whispered more to herself than to him.

That was when it hit him that he had not seen the real Natalie in years. The outgoing, fun-loving, bubbly, creative young girl who made his days miserable and so much fun was missing from the woman in front of him. He had seen hints of her: she was the one who ran out on her wedding, she was the one who sat in bed with him looking up her mom, she was the one in the water with him. That was not the town librarian she had become, the woman scared to let anyone see her scars and be hurt again.

"Except for the near-drowning, I liked her. How about we try on this trip to let her out some and see if she has grown up any?" He moved to sit on the same bench.

"She hasn't, and she never will. I don't want to be her." She turned her green eyes to him.

"How about this?" he proposed. "This week, you become Beckett. I want Beckett to be that part of you that you hide from everyone. Beckett doesn't let life get her down; Beckett doesn't think before she acts. I will be there to save her from drowning you."

"I don't know if I want to." Her eyes were on his.

"Beckett is up for anything. She's not scared." He took her hands into his so that she was no longer hugging her legs.

"You make it sound easy," she whispered.

"It will be easy, once you get used to being her again." He got up and pulled her to her feet. "Does Natalie or Beckett want to drive the boat?"

Once on her feet, she looked into his eyes, hers sparkling back at him, and she smiled. "Beckett does."

CHAPTER 9

As Sam placed the suitcases into the back of Natalie's SUV, Natalie chatted with his parents. They had been so nice to her over the past two days, she hated to be leaving. And from their extra hugs and come back soons, it seemed they hated to see her leave as well.

The days had been filled with stories of young Sam and his brothers. And not-so-subtle hints that the couple wanted them to date. From offering them to share a room to making sure they had a lot of alone time, they reminded her of her own dad and his reaction to her staying with Sam.

But now it was time to leave so she could finally meet her birth mother. Her nerves were starting to show as she gave the older Sullivans one last hug and climbed into the car beside Sam. She would let him drive again—she didn't want to think about driving while trying to figure out what to say to her mom.

She spent the day before trying to get past her nerves with Sam's help. Once he put the notion into her head that she could let her old self out a little, she tried. The boat ride had been amazing. She had never driven a boat before, and it was freeing to be able to drive anywhere, turn at any time. By the time it was over, she thought that

Sam was a little motion sick, but in true Sam fashion, he didn't say anything.

They had been able to go out again after supper in the boat, and she had promised not to drown him if he swam with her. He did of course, and she didn't even try to pants him, though it had been tempting. The water had been cool, and after a day in the sun, it had felt good.

She hadn't really meant to drown him that afternoon. She had planned to feed him the air she had in her mouth to him, but at that moment, she had thought it would be too much like a kiss and chickened out. Her hesitance had been what had almost drowned him. But through it all, she knew that even though she had her arms around his, it wasn't tightly. He could have freed himself at any moment, but he didn't. He just looked into her eyes under the water.

His anger annoyed her. He knew he could save himself. Was he mad about something else, and the incident had brought it to the surface? Maybe she had something to figure out herself this week.

Glancing over at him driving, she thought he looked pretty good in his khaki shorts and orange Landstad Tiger's T-shirt. Of course, he looked good in anything, it was super annoying. She loved that his hair was slightly longer than it should be and fell across his forehead. He had sunglasses on today, so she couldn't see his dark brown eyes.

"How long until we get there?" she asked, though she knew since she had looked it up after they had sat around the fire for a while the night before. His parents had tried everything to get them together.

"About two hours." He focused on the road ahead.

"I'm nervous. What if she sees me and knows it's me and she's mean, and I don't like her?" Natalie rambled as they drove.

"First, if you came from her, she is in no way going to be mean. Second, you are unrecognizable to people who actually knew you at ten, much less someone who maybe saw you at one day old. And third, she is going to love you," he assured her, which oddly worked to relax her a bit.

"Thanks. At least all that plastic surgery wasn't a waste. It's a great disguise." She laughed at her own painful past.

"No talk about surgeries or scars for the rest of the trip, Beckett." He was trying to use her new name more, get used to it. It was odd coming from him; he always made it sound like she was in trouble with his teacher voice.

"If you saw me naked, that is all you would be thinking about." She glanced across at him.

He slid his glasses off and met her eyes. "Scars would not be what I would be seeing if I saw you naked, Natalie."

Her mind was suddenly flooded with pictures of him kissing her scars all over her naked body, like he had the one on her arm on their walk. She could feel her cheeks grow hot with embarrassment.

"You called me Natalie." Heat flooded her at his words, but she forced herself to control it and called him out on saying her real name. Even if she couldn't take her eyes off his.

"I was talking to Natalie when I said it." He turned back to the road, and the car was left in a heavy silence.

His words reminded her that their trip was based on a make-believe relationship, but his words said that some of it wasn't pretend. Was he feeling what she was feeling? That pull toward him that had started when he carried her to his truck in the rainstorm? Had that pull started years before when she was too young to really know or care what it meant? All she knew was that she loved it when he had his arms around her and longed for his mouth on hers.

Miles rolled by as the silence between them grew heavier. At lunchtime, they stopped for a sit-down meal, as they were ahead of schedule and couldn't check into the B&B for another few hours even though they were less than an hour away.

They were sitting out on the patio of a restaurant neither had ever been to, looking at menus.

"Beckett."

"Sam?" she answered, trying to mimic his teacher voice but failing miserably, so she giggled.

"What are you having?" He smirked at her from over his menu.

"Something good." She didn't really answer his question since she hadn't decided yet.

"Are you nervous?" He closed his menu and put all his attention on her.

"Yes. What if I order wrong, and it's not very good?" She tried to break the tension between them and was rewarded with a laugh from him.

"I don't know if you have to worry too much," he said just as the waiter came back to the table and took their orders.

Watching the waiter leave, Natalie said, "Maybe I was nervous for no reason."

"Thank you, Natalie Beckett." He took her hand.

What was he talking about? "What for?"

"For letting me be a part of this."

"Right now, I can't imagine anyone else I would rather have with me. You seem to bring out some kind of bravery in me."

"You've always had that bravery in you. You're just learning how to let it out," he said.

"So you say." She couldn't tear her eyes from his. This was how she wanted to spend the rest of the day—just looking in his eyes and feeling special.

"So, this morning, my mom gave me this. She said you needed a ring if we were pretending to be married." Looking down, she saw he had a gold band he was slipping on to her finger.

It was a plain gold band, and it fit her perfectly. "Sam, I can't take your mom's wedding ring."

"It's not hers. It was her mother's." Holding her hand so she couldn't take it off, she just stared at it shining in the afternoon sun.

"Even worse, it's your grandma's ring!" She hated pretending being in a relationship, and she hated to bring a cherished family heirloom into her lies.

"No, she'll be happy you're wearing it. My grandfather was not in the picture long, so it'll be nice to give the ring another chance to be seen." He slid his thumb over the jewelry. A perfect fit.

"I don't know if I should feel honored that you're letting me use it or sad that this is all fake." She looked at the ring and his finger caressing it.

"Honored, Natalie. Just feel honored. Maybe one day you'll meet her. She would be so excited for our adventure." He picked up her hand and kissed the ring.

Feeling his lips on her finger, she wished she was really married to this man. Or even dating him. That would be enough for now.

"Thank you, Sam. It's beautiful," she whispered as the waiter came with their meals.

Sam let go of her hand so the man could put their plates down in front of them. In silence, they ate their meals, both concentrating on the food in front of them for a while. Natalie couldn't help but glance at the ring on her finger; it felt familiar, like she had been wearing it all her life. She should have thought about rings before she left him. Her dad's would have matched this one perfectly, and Sam could have worn that. Patrick hadn't worn it for years now, and if he did happen to remarry, he wouldn't wear it then either.

Her own engagement ring had been left at the church because it was with the best man for the ceremony. Which was for the best since she still didn't want to talk to Jason. At this point, she didn't know if she ever would.

"Do you like being a librarian?" he asked as he finished his burger.

"It's okay. I like when the school kids come in, and I like the quiet. Sometimes nobody comes in for hours, and I can just sit and read."

"Did you always want to be a librarian?" He pushed his plate away from him.

"No, I wanted to coach but not teach. I hadn't figured the whole thing out yet when the accident happened. That changed it all. Once I was a little better, I got my GED, and then I couldn't go to a lot of classes at that time. I could do the library science degree online, so I did that. I know Dad wanted me to get a degree. It worked better to get that degree, and I was able to get a job in Landstad right away."

"But you gave your two-week notice. Do you think they'll take you back?"

"I think so. They haven't hired anyone yet. I think I want to stay; I like it in town." She had missed it when she was gone.

Now being back was like being home, which was odd since she

had wanted nothing more than to get out before the accident. After she longed to go back. Even if she had planned to move once, she was nearly married, so it hadn't seemed real since she and Jason had dated long-distance for a long time. There had been so many things going through her head before the wedding, she hadn't even had time to dwell on actually leaving Landstad.

"I've learned to love it there. Just a fun little town. I like the other staff and the students. Now I've known them for most of their school careers and can't see myself walking away." He leaned back in his chair and looked at the traffic driving past the restaurant.

"Do you still like teaching? Or should I ask, do you still think about quitting?" His parents' words had bothered her. Sam had been a great teacher, even if she hadn't been a great student. To realize he almost stopped because of her hurt.

"I like it. I love teaching new kids every year that history is fun and exciting. It was only that one time I thought about quitting."

"You never taught me history that was exciting," she complained.

"You never listened to me," he informed her, and he was right.

"You're not wrong on that. I was an awful student," she admitted with a laugh.

"You just weren't challenged. Too smart for your own good." He laughed with her.

As they ate, they chatted about some of the kids she graduated with that they both knew and what they were up to. She was surprised that he kept in touch with so many of them and others he had taught over the years. In that way, he reminded her of her own father and the large circle of friends he has always had.

After lunch, the drive was easy and short. Too short. After a few minutes, the road signs actually said Birch Cove on them—seeing the numbers decrease at an alarming rate made her antsy—and soon enough, they were pulling into Birch Cove, the home of her mother. Nerves prevented her from speaking as soon as they hit city limits. All she could do was stare out the window at the town her mother grew up in and now lived.

Sam took her hand.

Pulling up in front of the building, Sam parked the car. She looked up at the big house that held her mother's law office and was amazed at the size of the place. It was in perfect shape for a building of that age, and the lawn and garden were also lovely.

Sam opened the door for her to get out and held out his hand to help her. Placing her hand in his, he pulled her to her feet and into a full hug. "Relax, Beckett," he whispered in her ear.

Nodding, she pulled out of his embrace, and he shut her door. Hand in hand, they walked to the front door together—they must look like a couple in love. Natalie hoped that they didn't look like a man with a petrified woman at his side because that was how she felt.

Sam opened the heavy front door to reveal a room full of people. Immediately, she could feel it was a workplace. At the reception desk sat a large muscular man who had a welcoming smile on his face. Without the smile, he would be intimidating. "Welcome to Hart Law Firm How can I help you?"

"We're here for the bed-and-breakfast. The website said to stop in here," Sam said to the man.

"Yes, we've been expecting you. I'll call Max to show you over there. You can just take a seat."

They sat on the bench along the wall and looked over the house. Natalie saw that the woodwork was in perfect condition and the hardwood floors sparkled. She also noticed that there was not a redhead in the room. A brunette and a blonde, but no redhead, like her mom. Had she really thought she would see her right away? That she would she see her at all?

She noticed a man walking down the stairway holding the hand of a little girl, about eight or nine. The little girl looked a bit like the father—their coloring was the same, but not the features. Did the little girl look like what Natalie used to look like? She couldn't always remember without a picture to remind her.

"Hello, Casey said you were here. I'm Max Valentine, and this is my daughter, Molly," he introduced them. "Did you have a good drive?"

"Yes, the drive was great. I'm Sam Sullivan, and this is my wife,

Beckett." Sam took over the conversation since Natalie was unable to speak.

"Nice to meet you. Beckett, that's an unusual name." Max looked at her closely.

"Her dad was a big English history buff, Thomas Beckett and all," Sam explained, showing off his knowledge of history.

"That's interesting. So, let's head across the road, and I'll show you around." Max ushered them from the law office.

"This is a gorgeous office," Sam commented as they descended the steps of the porch.

Natalie was following and trying to take everything in.

"It is," Max agreed. "I know my wife misses working here. She made it into what it is now."

"Where is she?" Sam asked, keeping up the conversation, oddly knowing exactly what she wanted to ask but couldn't.

"Here, but she's a judge, so she doesn't get to work in the office anymore." He waved down the street they were crossing. "She's at the courthouse a few blocks away."

"Wow, a judge. Has she been a judge a long time?" Sam took her hand since she was so busy looking around, her steps were slowing.

Sam was asking questions they knew the answers to, but Natalie was happy she was getting to hear it. Yes, she had read it, but hearing it was so much better.

"As long as we've been married, so around five years now. It seems like yesterday, but time does pass." Max was opening the door to the Victorian across the street from the law office. The house was not nearly as grand as the law firm.

"It wasn't yesterday, Dad. It was a long time ago," Molly informed Max with authority only an eight-year-old could pull off.

"It's an expression, Molly, I was just saying that I can remember very well when I met your mom." He smiled at his daughter.

"Mom says you didn't even notice her when you met."

"I noticed her later, and when I did, I didn't look away." Max then started pointing out the things Sam and Natalie would need to know about the house. Showing them the kitchen, dining room, and living room, he eventually showed them up the stairs to their bedroom.

Natalie bit her lip as she looked around the room with its one big bed. One big bed that they would have to share.

"I've put you guys in here. The room next door is empty as well if this one isn't comfortable. The one across the hall has guests coming tomorrow night. My sister-in-law and her husband are coming for a few days. It's my wife's birthday on Thursday." Max smiled at the couple.

"How old?" Sam asked.

CHAPTER 10

"The big four-zero. Zephyr coming is a surprise, so don't tell Della," Max said with a wink.

"I think Beckett needs a few minutes; she's getting over the flu." Sam hustled both Max and his daughter out of the room, leaving Natalie to digest what she had just heard.

Sitting down on the bed, Natalie tried to breathe. The small bits of information Max had provided were almost too much. Natalie wished she had known it before she came. The shock that the woman who had given her life had been just a girl at the time. She had turned sixteen the day Natalie had been born and given up for adoption. Sixteen. What had Natalie done when she was sixteen? Played sports and hung out with Hanna and Hazel. Maybe she had fallen for Henry, but maybe she was actually seventeen when that happened.

Della … The name played around in her head. Since the beginning, she had been Delphinea in Natalie's life. It was a long, difficult name, but it was the one they had for her. Della seemed to suit the redhead from the pictures more than the formal Delphinea.

When Sam brought in the suitcases, Natalie was still sitting on the bed, working things out in her mind. Once the door was closed and the bags were on the ground, Sam sat next to her. "I didn't realize she was so young."

"Me neither. It never crossed my mind. Why did I think she would have been in her twenties?" Natalie leaned into him.

"It changes things a little. Do you think she told him?" He wrapped his arm around her.

"I don't know. Maybe she doesn't want to see me?" Natalie had to stop herself from crawling onto his lap and letting him comfort her.

"Didn't you get a letter once saying that she wanted to see you?"

"Yes, but that was years ago. She wasn't even married then," she realized.

"Well, we're here now, and you don't have to tell her who you are. Just have a few fun days in a new town." He kissed her forehead.

"Maybe we can stay long enough to see her. Just once." She pulled out of his arms, not wanting him to feel uncomfortable, even if she still wanted his comfort for herself.

"I told Max that you were on the softball team in high school, so he's getting his other daughter, and you're going to show them how to pitch. The other daughter wants to learn how." Sam got up from the bed.

After getting their stuff sorted out in the room, they headed outside to see if the Valentines were out of their house. Natalie spotted them before Sam did, playing in the large open yard beside the house. As they walked over, Natalie saw the other girl looked like her sister. They must be Max's from a previous relationship since Della and Max hadn't been married all that long.

Molly saw them first and ran toward them. She introduced her sister and remembered their names to tell her sister. Lilly, the older girl, was more subdued than her little sister.

Soon, Natalie had Lilly pitching well for her first time. Since the actual pitching in softball was different from baseball, it took time to get the basics down. It had been so long since Natalie had actually picked up a softball, she had to remind herself. At first, she had Sam catching the balls and Molly trying to hit them, but soon it became apparent that Lilly wasn't that good with the pitching, so Sam started helping Molly catch the balls that came her way. Max had moved from the outfield, where Molly was hitting the ball to, and was now leaning against the house, watching and encouraging his girls.

Natalie was having so much fun watching Sam and Molly catch the wayward balls. He was so good with kids, she realized. He knew what to say and when to say it. Maybe that was why she was so drawn to him—because he was so kind to everyone.

The two adults were trading insults as they played. Natalie teased Sam's ability to catch, and Sam joked about Natalie's ability to catch the balls he threw back. Neither said anything about the way the girl pitched, except encouragements.

She had actually forgotten why she was there, playing with the two children, when Molly let out a scream and ran toward where her dad stood. Turning, Natalie got weak in the knees at the woman Molly threw herself at. The short redhead had to be Della Hart. She actually looked just like her picture on the internet, minus the black robe. Red curly hair in a style that looked haphazard but wasn't at all. She was wearing a straight skirt and a green blouse, and the heels she wore made her head come up to her husband's chin. Without them, she would be close to five feet tall.

Feeling Sam wrap his arms around her from behind, she leaned into him. Staring at the woman who was supposed to have given her life, she wondered how it would be possible. The redhead was her complete opposite. Della's red hair shone in the sun, so different from Natalie's black tresses. Add in the height discrepancy since Natalie was closer to Della's husband as far as the color of their skin. Natalie looked down at her olive arm, then glanced at the pale redhead. There was no way this was her mother.

She felt Sam pushing her from behind toward the little family greeting each other after a day apart. Hugs and kisses for all, chatter about what happened. A smiling Della Hart looked up at the couple as they came close enough. Natalie almost stopped breathing as she saw her own green eyes looking at her. Sam was holding her tight, so she wouldn't fall down.

Could they tell?

"You guys must be Sam and Beckett. Thank you for playing with the girls," Della stated with a wide smile, her eyes looking right at Natalie as she spoke. Could she tell who she was? Did she want her to be there if she did?

"Hello, Judge Valentine," Sam said.

It was a good thing he could talk.

Natalie watched the woman laugh. "Judge Connor Hart and Mrs. Max Valentine, but you can call me Della."

"Della, then. It was fun teaching the kids. But it was mostly Beckett. She was a pitcher in high school. I figured if anyone could teach Lilly, it was her." Sam pulled back from Natalie to make her stand on her own.

"What do you two do?" Della asked.

"I'm a teacher, and she's a librarian," Sam supplied.

Natalie knew she could have answered that one. Why couldn't he leave her the easy ones?

"How are you liking the B&B?" Della looked at Natalie again.

"We are," Sam answered again.

"Aunt Mae used to live there, but she's in heaven with my mommy," Molly said from beside her mom. Natalie watched Lilly poke her with an elbow.

Squatting down to her level, Natalie said, "My mom's in heaven too."

Molly stepped closer to her. "My mommy died when I was three."

"My mom died when I was six," Natalie admitted.

"Do you have a new mommy? I do." The girl looked up at Della, who rested a hand on her small shoulder.

"No, but I think maybe soon I might get one. I just have my dad, but he was pretty nice to me. Do you like your new mommy?" Natalie confided in the little girl.

"Yes. Daddy too. He lets me sleep with them sometimes." She giggled, making the adults smile.

"That's pretty nice of him."

The girl nodded and just looked at Natalie. Natalie analyzed the little girl, realizing she was as adopted as Natalie herself was. She and her new sister had a lot in common.

"What is that?" The little girl pointed at Natalie.

Looking down, she realized her shorts had ridden up, and one of her scars was showing. A bad one. "That is a scar, Molly. Do you have any scars?" She pulled her shorts down her leg cover it back up.

"Yes, I fell off my bike and got a good one on my knee." She pointed it out on her little leg.

"I was in a car accident. I got some good ones too," Natalie said, feeling Sam touch her shoulder in comfort. They had agreed not to talk about the accident, but here it was. Always present.

"Can I see?" Molly asked eagerly.

"No, they're not as nice-looking as yours." Natalie touched the knee with the faint scar.

"Please." Blue eyes pressed her.

"Okay." She pulled up the short's hem higher so the little girl could see the jagged scar where a piece of glass had been embedded in her skin.

Watching the little girl's eyes get wide as she looked at the red puckered skin that looked like it might still have stitches in it today. The little girl reached out and touched it.

Natalie wanted to pull away but didn't want to frighten the little girl.

"It feels weird. How did you get it?" the girl asked.

"I was in a big car accident. When you think you don't need to wear your seat belt, just remember this scar. I wasn't wearing one that day," Natalie explained.

"You have to wear a seat belt in the car, Beckett, it's the law," said the kid of a judge.

"I know. Now I wear one every time," Natalie promised.

"Do you have any more scars?" Molly asked, looking at her other leg, the one that didn't have any as obvious as the one Molly had touched.

"Yes, but I'll not show you anymore. Just this one. Lilly, did you want to touch it?" She turned to the girl on the other side of her mother. Not wanting to leave the other sister out.

"No." Lilly backed up a little.

Natalie had been surprised at Molly's reaction to the scar, but Lilly's was the more common reaction.

"You guys should come over for supper, in thanks of helping the girls." Max had slipped his arms around his wife as Natalie had spoken to Molly.

"No, we couldn't impose." Sam helped Natalie to her feet.

"We'll not take no for an answer." Della pulled herself from her husband's embrace, and for a second, Natalie thought she was going to hug her until she turned and walked toward the front door of the law office away from everyone.

Sam took Natalie's hand and followed the shorter woman into the building. Once inside, Max took over, leading them to the back kitchen as Della went upstairs to change. She and Sam sat on the stools at the island as Max started to cook. When Della came into the kitchen, she sat down on the remaining stool and watched her husband cook.

Looking over at the younger couple, she explained, "I don't cook, so Max does all the cooking now. I don't even pretend anymore. Not that I pretended for long."

"You could pretend to get drinks, beautiful," Max said to his wife.

With a smile at him, the woman laughed and got up to get beverages for everyone. Soon the kids wandered off to play, leaving the adults to talk.

"Do you live here?" Natalie looked over at the quiet office.

"Yes, we live upstairs, but the kitchen is down here. It's a little inconvenient, but I like it here still." Della took out glasses from the cabinet.

"Is the upstairs as nice as the downstairs?" Sam asked.

"Oh yes. The entire house is gorgeous. I love it here." Della set the glasses in front of the younger couple.

"I bet it is. It must have cost a fortune," Natalie said.

"It's been in my family forever. It's called the Connor Mansion. I just had to fix it up since it had sat empty for years," Della explained. "It took over a year.

Natalie looked around and wondered what it could have possibly looked like empty. After seeing the office full of activity, she could barely believe it could ever have been empty?

"How long have you two been married?" Max asked from in front of the stove.

"Just recently tied her down." Sam pulled her close to him.

She went willingly into his arms.

"Have you known each other a long time?" Della asked.

"We met years ago, but we got together more recently. We're from a small town where everybody knows everybody," Sam said.

"What he doesn't say is that he was my teacher when I was in high school. During my senior year, he taught history, boring history," she said with a laugh.

"Not boring, you just didn't pay attention," he replied into her hair.

His touch and teasing made her smile. The man had a way of knowing when she needed him and was there for her. Sam, who could make her laugh or cry at a word. Sam, who was going to be sleeping next to her in the next few hours. Sam, who was stealing her heart a little at a time.

"So, how long have you been together now? How did it happen?" Della asked with interest, bringing her back and making her realize she had no idea how to answer.

CHAPTER 11

Feeling Natalie stiffen in his arms, Sam answered for her. "Last year, at this time, Natalie almost got married but took off before the ceremony. I caught her in the parking lot and took her home. We've been together ever since."

It was the truth after all, just a different time. Even as he said the words, he realized that they had been together ever since the wedding. Before that, they hadn't seen each other in years, and now he didn't know how he was going to go back to not having her around.

"How romantic." Della looked at the two of them.

"It is. We're on a sort of honeymoon now." Sam took advantage of the situation and kissed Natalie's temple.

The conversation went back to his teaching and history, something Max also enjoyed. He told them a little about Birch Cove's past, including about the Conners and how they had come to own half the town once.

All the while, Natalie seemed to be lost in her own thoughts. If she was even listening, he didn't know. But when Della said her name, she jumped a little, and he tightened his hold on her, hoping the other couple hadn't noticed.

"Beckett?"

"What? I was daydreaming, I guess. Sorry," Natalie mumbled.

"I was just saying I was sorry about Molly asking about the scars. She's very precocious," Della explained of her youngest child.

"That's okay, I usually get Lilly's reaction to them. Most kids find my scars scary, some adults also. I try to keep them covered." Natalie touched her leg that Molly had touched without seeming to notice it.

"Was the accident bad?" Max asked from the kitchen.

Sam took over because Natalie shouldn't have to. "Yes, Beckett barely survived it, and others didn't."

Della and Max seemed to have noticed that Natalie had gone pale and let the subject fall as the girls ran into the room, fighting about something and further breaking up the conversation.

Once Max was finished making the chicken dish, he was making sure they all gathered around the table to eat. Sam looked around the table. The girls were eating without the complaining, which wasn't expected. Max and Della were sitting side-by-side, and at one point, Max leaned over and gave his wife a kiss on the cheek that made her giggle.

With the meal done and the dishes put in the dishwasher, Sam and Natalie excused themselves and went back to the B&B across the road. Sam knew the night had to come to an end but was sad when it did. Natalie had become relaxed with the couple and their children—she was able to be herself. He knew she was enjoying herself and learning more and more about her mother. Della had talked about her three sisters and their families a little, two of which lived within a few miles of Della. Some about her youth growing up in town, too.

When Della had said she had skipped grades in school to graduate early, he was reminded of how bored Natalie used to be in school. The younger woman must have inherited her brains from Della. When Natalie talked about sports, Della had admitted she was no good at them, so that must have come from her father.

Once he had shut the door behind them at the B&B, she started talking about their day. She was giddy with excitement over her new knowledge of her mother and for what she had learned about herself.

To Sam, it seemed she had learned more in the last few hours than the twenty-four years prior. Enjoying the chatter, he just let her ramble on, recapping events he was right beside her for.

When they had made it to their bedroom, she suddenly became quiet, and the single bed was all he could think about suddenly. That and all the things that they could do in that bed that they shouldn't do.

"I'll sleep on the floor." Sam picked up his suitcase.

"No, I will. You've done so much for me to sleep on the floor. I will." She dug through her bag, but whether she was actually looking for something or avoiding looking at him he didn't know.

"So, you think your back would be fine sleeping on the hard floor?" He looked at her back, mostly because it was facing him.

"I'll survive." She continued digging through her bag, not looking up.

"No, you'll be in pain. And maybe in pain tomorrow also. I will sleep on the floor." He headed out the door to the bathroom, not letting her argue anymore.

As he brushed his teeth, he tried hard to put her back in the category of student, but he couldn't. She was no longer that girl in the back row of senior history. She was Natalie now. And it was Natalie with whom he wanted to share a bed. But he was determined not to let anything happen on this trip. Her emotions were stretched to the limit as it was, and she didn't need him confusing her more.

Changing into the basketball shorts and T-shirt he had brought, he headed out to the bedroom. Dropping his bag on the ground near the door, he saw she was sitting on the bed, but she had changed into the short shorts and the tank top she had worn on the deck. In the light of the room, he was able to see the scar that came out of the top of her tank top between her breasts, but it was the breasts that had his full attention. They were clearly visible beneath the tight tank top. He could almost feel them in his hands as her nipples suddenly became visible under the thin material.

Before he could say anything, she jumped off the bed, grabbed a small bag, and rushed past him. Not a word was said as she went.

Sam was plugging in his phone when she came back into the

bedroom, just as annoyed as when she had left. He watched her flounce through the room and plop down on the bed on top of the blankets, the same spot she had been sitting in before going to the bathroom.

"Can we just be adults about this, Sam? Sleep in the bed?" Picking up her phone, she scrolled through it and ignored him.

"I can sleep on the floor." He looked in the closet for more blankets.

"You probably can, but you can also sleep in the bed." She didn't look up from her phone.

"And make you sleep on the floor?" Nothing in there, so he turned to her.

"I think the bed is big enough for two." She finally looked up at him and tapped on the pillow beside her.

"I don't think that would be a good idea, Natalie." Sam sighed.

"I promise not to touch you if you promise not to touch me. Just sleep. I am so tired I can't think of anything I would rather do anyway." She tapped the pillow again.

Knowing it was a bad idea, Sam walked around the bed and pulled back the blanket, crawling in beside her. He wasn't going to let her see that she was having any effect on him. That she turned him on. That he was having a hard time trusting himself around her.

Laying on his side, facing away from her, he wondered if she was still on her phone. But he didn't want to roll over and find out. Staring at the wall, he felt her shifting now and then in the bed, and before long, he felt her get out of the bed. Suddenly, the room went dark around him. It was even worse feeling her climb back into bed in the dark room. All he wanted to do was turn over and pull her into his arms where she belonged. Instead, he stayed looking at the opposite wall in the darkness.

"Do you think she's my mother?" she asked into the dark room.

Rolling to his back at her words, he looked at the dark ceiling. "Yes, she reminds me of you. Just little things."

"Not looks. We look completely different." She held up her hand

and arm in the dark room. He couldn't not think she was looking at her skin tone, which was not the same as Della's.

"You're right. Your body type is not hers, but your eyes are. And the quick laugh—you both don't hesitate to laugh," he replied in the dark, not mentioning how close the laughs were to each other in tone and timbre.

"She's nice, though."

"Are you going to tell her?"

"I don't know yet. What if no one knows, and I wreck her secret? It's her secret, not mine."

"Natalie, I can't believe that if it is a secret, she wouldn't want to know who you are anyway. I'm sure she thinks about you."

"It was a long time ago, and she was young."

"Not that young, Natalie." He dealt with sixteen-year-olds all the time—she did not.

"I've been trying to remember what I did when I turned sixteen. I think I was grounded for stealing a bottle of wine from my dad and getting drunk with Hanna while he was off shopping for my birthday present. So, instead of spending the day with my friends, I spent it alone in my room. Except I snuck out and wandered around town until Dad found me and grounded me again." Natalie went silent. "She had me."

"Everyone lives a different life. You don't know how she got pregnant or why she gave you up. Only she knows the answers."

"I wonder why she adopted her kids instead of having more?" she questioned.

"Sometimes when you want kids later in life, it doesn't happen," he guessed. He had no idea what would make her give up one child for adoption and then adopt two others.

"Maybe. Maybe there's more to it," Natalie said, more into the night than to him.

"Good night, Natalie." He turned back away from her.

"Good night, Sam. I promise not to touch you." He could tell she was smiling as she said the words.

It ended up taking more than an hour for Sam to finally fall asleep. Within minutes he knew Natalie was asleep, as her breathing evened out and she stopped moving, so he rolled onto his back and stared at the ceiling. Four nights in this bed together. Four nights of having to fight pulling her into his arms. Four nights of her breathing beside him. Four nights of trying to keep his body under control with her so close.

CHAPTER 12

Pain once again dragged Natalie from sleep. Today's pain was eased by turning over and relieving the pressure on her spine. Except now, she was face-to-face with Sam Sullivan, still sleeping since his breathing was steady and even. His eyes lids hid the brown eyes she liked so much, his hair was tussled and sticking out from his head, fanned out on his pillow. The sheet had slipped down, and his arm was lying on top of the blankets. At some point, he had removed the T-shirt she was sure he had been wearing when he had gotten into bed. It was maybe too hot in the room overnight. He looked at peace.

Dawn's first rays seeped into the window at the foot of the bed, and it made him more visible with every passing minute. She should get up and leave him alone to sleep as long as possible, but the warmth of the bed and the nearness of Sam kept her where she was.

She flipped the blankets off because the heat in the room was too much, then she tucked her arm under her pillow, so she could prop her head up a little before placing the other hand on his chest to feel that he was breathing. Oddly, she noticed that her hand was darker than his tanned chest. For a moment, she wondered about the rest of her genes. Where did they come from?

Her eyes drew back to his face, and she saw that his brown eyes were open and looking at her. Neither moved as they looked at each other, but she could feel his heart beating faster. Just like hers was.

His hand that was on top of the blanket moved, and she felt it gently touch the scar on her chest, the big one. It ran from about two inches from her throat down through her breast to below her rib cage. The doctor had said that it would always look like it did right now.

His finger started at the top and slid slowly down the scar until it hit the top of her tank top, then he pushed the fabric down, pulling her shirt with it. She had been watching his eyes that were watching his finger as they darkened with desire. Soon his head leaned down, and she felt his lips on the top of her scar, then they too followed the path south.

When the shirt wouldn't go down anymore, she felt his tongue on the scar, leaving a trail of moisture as it came back to the top. Natalie shivered at the sensation. No man had used her scars to turn her on, but Sam did. Once at the top, he nuzzled into her neck and kissed her where her pulse beat, causing a moan to escape her throat.

Sliding kisses down her arm to the scar he had kissed just a few days before, he rained kisses on the spot again. All Natalie could do was watch him and pray he didn't stop touching her. When his eyes sought out hers, the desire she saw made her gasp. As their gazes held, she gave a slight nod of approval. Yes, she wanted this, and it melted her heart that he asked.

His lips returned once again to the scar on her arm for one more light kiss, then he shifted slightly and took her pert nipple into his hot mouth. The sensation of his suckling through the thin fabric made her moan again, and her hand went into his dark hair to hold his mouth to her breast, just in case he tried to pull away.

Rolling onto her back, she pulled him with her, but he took advantage of the move to suckle the other breast. Freeing her hands out of his hair, she pulled at the hem of her tank top—she needed his lips on more of her skin. Her bare skin. When her shirt had come off, she was rewarded with a pleased sigh. His lips immediately repeated what he had done with her breast, but this time with no barrier.

She ran her hands over the muscles on his bare shoulders, loving the feel of his smooth skin. The sun was casting just enough glow in the room that she could see him as his lips left her breasts and continued down the scar between them.

By the time he made it to the bottom of the large scar, she was panting, and her body was buzzing with need. His mouth skittered across her stomach to a six-inch puckered scar. He trailed his fingers over the rough edges, then ran kisses over the ugly wound.

Looking up at her until their eyes met and held, he whispered, "Your body is gorgeous, Natalie. Every scar reminds me how lucky I am to be here with you. How close this came to not happening. How much I nearly missed. That life is fragile, and I can't take anything for granted. That I need to cherish you every opportunity I can get." Then he went back to her body and kissed his way back up, but this time his lips ended on hers. The kiss he gave her was soft and delicate, just like the kisses he had planted all over her body.

That was when she took control of the situation and ran her hands up his body and into his hair, pulling his head to hers in a hungry kiss. His need was as demanding as hers when she slid her tongue into his hot and waiting mouth. She swallowed his groan of delight and let her hands run the length of his body, down his strong shoulders to his abs that didn't end until she hit the waistband of those sexy shorts.

Without missing a beat, she slid her fingers beneath his shorts and cupped his firm bare ass in her hands, loving that it made him groan in her mouth as she ground her core into his straining erection.

His hand skimmed slowly down her body as they kissed. He cupped her breasts, making her arch her back in encouragement. That was all he needed as his thumbs brushed over her peeked nipples, causing the ache in her core to intensify.

All she could do was moan in his mouth as the fingers left her breasts and slid down her stomach, slipping into her panties. Just where she wanted him, her hands fell from his body as he shifted.

Cupping her core, she whimpered, causing his lips to leave hers. Gently kissing down her neck, his finger slipped into her. Her eyes gently closed, and the sensations shooting through her body as his fingers started to move caused her breath to catch. His lips had once again found her breasts, and his tongue movements were perfectly matching what his thumb was doing to her clit. Her orgasm was building slowly until he slipped a finger into her core. Instantly, she was rocking and moaning to the rhythm his hand had set. When he slid a second finger inside her, her entire world broke apart, and she was lost in the amazing feelings of her body pulsing around his hand.

Panting and unable to move, she watched him kiss her scars again while she got her heart and body back under control. The light kisses didn't seem like anything, but they made her body hum with excitement. As her energy returned, she ran her hands over his perfect body once more, loving the feel of him. His back, his chest, his great abs, and finally into the shorts, but this time she stroked his straining cock, making him groan. He was larger than she had expected, but that only sent a shiver of excitement through her. Her core was still pulsing from her past orgasm, and she was already getting excited for the next one.

Sam's lips hovered over hers, but there was disappointment in his eyes. "We can't have sex. I don't have any condoms."

"I'm on the pill." Closing the space between them, she kissed him, pushing off his shorts and underwear until she was able to see his naked body. He made her mouth water. He was gorgeous.

She raised her hips to help him remove the last remaining clothing she wore, the shorts and panties that hadn't seemed to be in his way earlier. As she watched his eyes sweep over her body, she had the sudden urge to cover herself, but his words stopped her. "God, you're beautiful. Just as beautiful as I always thought you would be."

Shifting over her, he nuzzled her neck and settled between her thighs. Lifting his head, he questioned, "Does this hurt your back?"

All she could do was shake her head and kiss him—her back was the last thing she was feeling right now. She loved that he remembered her pain when all she could think about was having him inside her. Shifting her hips, she pressed her bare core against his cock and ground against him.

Groaning, he shifted his hips, and in one smooth motion, he slid into her.

Moaning at the sensation, she let her head fall back onto the pillow. All she could feel was him filling her. Then he began to move, slow and steady, like she was too delicate to push too hard. The steady in and out of his cock was amazing, but she needed more, faster.

The strain of his face told her how hard it was for him to control himself, that he was taking care of her. No matter what he was feeling or wanting.

Wrapping her legs around him, she pushed herself up and kissed his cheek. "Harder, Sam. I won't break."

"I don't want to hurt you," he said, not changing the rhythm he had set.

"Nothing you will do will hurt me," she promised, smiling.

His concerned eyes locked with hers. "Are you sure?"

Running her hands down his chest and grabbing his hips, she grinned. "Fuck me, Sam. Hard."

That was all he needed as the dam broke, and he picked up speed. His cock slammed into her, making her toes curl until she was screaming his name, telling him to never stop. Her orgasm came quickly, and he still pumped in and out of her in hard, easy strokes.

Then he shifted, and she was coming again, but this time he was coming with her. His groans melted with hers as her body spasmed around him. Sam rolled off her and lay beside her, but he grabbed her hand and pulled it to his mouth and kissed her fingers. "Anything hurt?" he asked when he could breathe again, his worry always there.

"I don't know. Pain is not a feeling I have at this moment." Grinning, she brushed a lock of hair off his damp forehead.

"Me either."

Silently, they both lay looking at the ceiling, hands linked and still breathing heavily. Rolling onto his side toward her, he waited for her to do the same. Once she did, he touched her cheek with his thumb. "What are you thinking?"

Biting her lip, she said, "You first."

"I've wanted you for days. I wanted to wait until we got back home, so I could ask you on a date, then I was going to get you in bed. But I'm happy my plan didn't work." He smiled.

"Me too. It's only been five days, but I've been with you every moment of those days." She held up a hand with all fingers spread out. He slid his fingers between them to hold her hand.

"Would you go out with me when we get back to Landstad? To a movie and eat something?" he asked.

She smiled at him. "Only if you'll take me home afterward."

"I don't want to assume." He pulled their joined hands and kissed hers.

"Assume, Mr. Sullivan." She laughed.

"Beckett." He chuckled, rolling her onto her back with him laying on top of her.

Laughing as he kissed her neck, she pushed at him. "I have to take a shower."

"Do you want to go first?" He kissed her shoulder blade. "Do you want to go second?" He kissed the pulse in her neck. "Or do you want to go together?" He kissed her cheek.

"My answer is C, Mr. Sullivan. Always C." And she kissed his mouth.

CHAPTER 13

Sam pulled Natalie into his arms and nuzzled her neck until she giggled. He had found out she was ticklish by accident early in the day, and he loved to hear her giggle when he touched her neck. It had taken no time to get used to touching her.

"Sam, quit distracting Beckett. It's her turn!" Max yelled from across the yard. Looking up, he saw that all were looking at him and Natalie. Letting her go, he went back to his position as catcher. They were playing kickball, or some form of kickball.

Watching Natalie's butt as she got ready to kick the ball that Max was rolling her way, he remembered that butt in the shower this morning. If she had any regrets about starting a relationship with him, he had yet to see any signs of it. She was as enthusiastic about being together as he was.

Once they made it out of the shower, Della had been making breakfast for them. Sheepishly they had come down the stairs as she was just finishing making French toast. Della had stayed and chatted with them as they ate and invited them over for a birthday get-together in the afternoon at the mansion across the road. Della told them it was just going to be her family coming.

That left just enough time for him and Natalie to go for a long walk after breakfast and tour the town hand in hand. It was Wednesday morning in July, so the town was busy with everyday business, and it reminded him a little of Landstad. Half of him wanted to stay there forever with her and not let the real world into their lives, and half of him wanted to take her back and announce she was his to their town. He really didn't think anyone would care that she had been his student or even that she had almost gotten married last week. They would talk about it for a few days, then it would be replaced by the next big thing.

Late in the morning, during their walk, she got a phone call from her dad. Stopping outside an accounting firm, she leaned against the brick wall and chatted with the man. As she talked, she had left her hand bunching his shirt, pulling him closer to her.

With his hands against the cool brick, he listened to his friend on the phone. After all, if she hadn't wanted him listening, she wouldn't have pulled him close.

"Nobody's really saying anything anymore, at least not to me. But maybe they're just waiting for you to come home," Patrick was saying.

"I expect people will start talking when I get back. Hopefully it'll be behind my back, so I don't have to listen to it." She slid her hand under his shirt and rested it on his chest.

"Mia said that the talk has really died down there. Greg Miller called and asked if you wanted to stay at the library." Greg Miller was her boss and the person she needed to talk to in order to get her job back.

"What did you say?" Her hand stopped moving.

"I might have overstepped the boundary, but I said you wanted to stay. Was I wrong?" Her dad sounded hesitant.

"No, not wrong. I want to stay." Her hand started moving again, and he kissed her neck and watched her bite her lip to keep from giggling.

"Good. I want you to stay. But I think you need to find a place of your own now," her dad said.

Her eyes met his over the phone. "Because you don't want me

there anymore or because you have some kid who is eyeing my room?"

"Of course, I want you, Natalie," her dad protested. "But you need to stand on your own two feet. This seems like the perfect opportunity for you to do that."

"And?" Natalie pushed, eyes still on Sam's.

"And maybe Faith has agreed to move in, and we need your room for one of the boys," Patrick admitted.

"Was that so hard, Dad?" she asked with a laugh and a sparkle in her green eyes.

"No, I should have done it long ago."

"Yes, you should have. Stringing that woman along for years, Patrick. You should know better," she scolded her dad.

"I know," Patrick said, almost too quiet for Sam to hear.

"I'll call Ruth and see if she has anything for me to rent."

Ruth was a part of her book club, but Sam really didn't know her except she worked at the insurance office downtown. Not the one he had insurance through, though, the other one.

"Don't rush on my account," Patrick protested.

"I *will* rush for you because you drag your feet. Get them settled before school starts again. If Ruth doesn't have anything right now, I'll find a friend to stay with," she said into the phone and then pointed at Sam.

"I really don't want to put you out," Patrick was saying as Sam was thinking about her moving in with him. It didn't scare him at all. It didn't even feel like it was too soon.

"You might be doing me a favor. We'll talk when I get back," Natalie said, smiling at Sam.

"Love you, Natalie."

"Love you, Dad." And she hung up the phone.

Lowering his lips to hers, he kissed her right there in the middle of busy Main Street. Pulling back, he asked, "Are you imoving in with me?"

"I am not. I have a few options before I'm forced to move in with you … but you do have a nice shower." She kissed him before he could respond.

Now they were on opposing teams of kickball. As the kickball came rolling toward her, she ran at it and kicked it with a fraction of the strength she would usually use. The ball flew about ten feet and landed at the feet of a six-year-old boy, who just looked at it as it rolled away from him. Natalie took off toward first base on the slowest run he had ever seen.

After their walk, they had gone to the birthday party. To their surprise, there was a crowd. Or at least the start of one, despite the woman only having two sisters. With them, their spouses, and their kids, there were a lot more people than Sam had expected. After a lunch of hotdogs on the grill, they had picked teams for kickball: girls vs. boys. Each team had a handful of adults and a few kids. The game was geared toward the little kids, and anyone over twelve had to restrain themselves.

On her slow run to the base, she almost tripped over a two-year-old redheaded girl who had wandered into the playing field heading toward her mom. Scooping up the little girl, she kept going, watching them scramble for the ball until an adult had it—then she was running full out. A dark-haired man had the ball and threw it to get her out. Tucking the girl under her arm to protect her from the flying object, she dodged the ball and made it to the base with a cheer and a little dance. Della's red-haired daughter, who was on second base, joined in.

Sam looked around the group and was struck by how much the sisters looked alike. Even though one had blonde hair, they all looked the same. Though Natalie looked nothing like them, even if she still had their noses, she would still stick out from the group. None of the sisters were taller than 5'4", and that was only because Della was wearing tall heels, even while playing. Natalie was nearly six feet tall in comparison.

But no matter what the outside looked like, they all had the same fun-loving personality. They all loved to tease and make fun of everyone. No one was safe. Della's nephew, who was around seventeen, was teased about everything from the girls he might like to missing an easy catch, sometimes even by his own mother.

Della's sister Evie's turn was next, and she kicked the ball with all her might, and her son went after the ball on a run. Both Zoe and Natalie took off around the bases with all the speed they had, and to his surprise, Zoe could get some speed. The ball was coming back to him, and Zoe was coming at him.

Before he knew what was happening, she pushed right past him as the ball was thrown at her, missing her by an inch. But in the process, she took Sam to the ground. Catching her in his arms so that she didn't slide onto the grass, he was oddly on the ground with her in his arms. She looked up at him and started to laugh. His breath stopped as he watched her eyes sparkle in her merriment, just like Natalie's, only in a different color—hers were brown.

The game stopped to make sure everyone was okay. Zoe insisted she was fine due to Sam catching her. Sam only had a few grass stains and a sore behind, but that would be fine in a few minutes. What would take longer was the realization that Natalie was a part of these people. This was where she was from, and they would accept her in a heartbeat if she allowed it.

Just as Zoe was being lifted over the shoulder of her husband, who was going to take her inside to see if she was really okay, a car pulled up to the curb. Just like in Landstad, everyone turned to see. To Sam's surprise, another redhead climbed out of the passenger door. He was starting to have a hard time keeping them straight.

Zoe pounded on her husband's back, yelling to let her down, and the three sisters went to hug the new one. Natalie came to stand beside Sam, slipping her hand into his. He pulled her, so she was in his arms.

With a shrug, both Sam and Natalie decided that the game was over since once the hugs were done between the sisters, the newcomer's husband walked around the car carrying a two-year-old in his arms. They received the same hugs and handshakes from the men. Zoe, who had managed to get free, pulled the toddler boy from his arms as Della went into the back of the car to take out a car seat that must have contained a baby.

Looking up, Della noticed them standing off to the side and waved them over. It felt odd going over to the big family greeting, but Sam knew she had to go over there and meet her new relatives. This might be her only chance.

"I'm sorry we forgot about you guys. My sister Zephyr is here with the kids," she said, and the tall black man cleared his throat. "And Zachary, of course."

They nodded at him, and he smiled at them. In a smooth southern accent, he said, "Hi, Zachary Wainwright. That's my wife, Zephyr. Zion is with Zoe, and the baby is Zelda."

"Sam and Beckett Sullivan." He indicated to himself and Natalie.

"Nice to meet you. They get a little crazy. I'm not used to it," the man informed them as if sensing they were uncomfortable.

"Us either." Natalie spoke for the first time.

Della turned to them, holding a six-month-old baby in her arms. "This is Zelda. Zelda, this is Beckett." Oddly, she didn't introduce Sam to the baby, just her. In fact, she didn't even look his way.

"Hello, Zelda. How are you?" Natalie asked the baby with a smile, shaking the tiny hand.

Sam looked from her to the baby and back again. The skin tone was far closer to what Natalie's had been in the baby pictures Patrick had displayed in his house. And even the button nose was there. For a moment, he knew this is what Natalie's babies would look like, or far closer than the other kids there that day. That was if she could have them. It was a punch in the gut to see it.

"Zephyr and Zachary are staying at the B&B tonight. Also, they always stay over there," Della informed them.

The new arrival walked up to her sister and put her arms around her with a smile, and said, "Happy Birthday, Della."

"Thanks," Della said, but she didn't smile with her sister.

"We stay at the B&B because that's where I fell in love with Zachary." Her southern accent was as pronounced as her husband's— far different from any of her three sisters.

"Liar, you were already in love with me long before we got here." Zachary slipped an arm around his wife.

"It's still very special to me," Zephyr said, looking at her husband with love in her eyes.

"Beckett here is a librarian," Della informed her.

"Really," was all Zephyr said. Not expanding on why it was something that needed to be said.

"Yes." Natalie didn't know what else to say about it. Her job was pretty boring most of the time.

The crowd was starting to disband. Evie took the baby from Della and went into the house with Zoey. Soon Zephyr and Zachary headed into the house also, and the kids soon followed, looking for something to eat.

Soon it was just Della, Max, Beckett, and Sam on the lawn, watching the last of the people wander into the house after the new arrivals.

"We should go and let you be with your family," Natalie said from his arms.

"No, you come and join us," Della insisted, and Sam watched Max pull her into his arms and whisper something in her ear.

"Supper is about ready, and it's Della's birthday party. She would really like you two to be there. She doesn't do much for her birthday usually," Max said with a lazy smile.

Feeling the tension leave Natalie's body at his words, Sam said, "We can stay for a little while. But can you give us a minute?"

"Sure, see you inside." Max let his wife go from the embrace but took her hand to lead her to their house.

Sam and Natalie watched them walk across the yard hand in hand and then walk up the stairs. They were chatting quietly as they walked, and at the top of the stairs, Max pulled her into his arms and kissed her. Sam could hear her laugh when they separated.

"Did you want to go?" He pulled Natalie in for a hug.

"They remind me of my mom and dad, that's all," she explained from his shoulder.

"They kind of are, Natalie," he whispered to her.

"No, I mean that's how Patrick was with Lara. I remember that. They were very touchy-feely. I wonder if he'll be that way with Faith?"

"Do you want him to be?" he asked, wondering if she was really okay with her dad's relationship.

"I hope he is. Then I'll know he loves her," Natalie replied on a sigh.

Just holding her, he realized that was the kind of relationship he wanted with Natalie. To be able to sense her moods and do exactly what she needed him to do. To do things to just make her happy.

CHAPTER 14

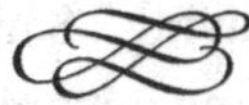

WALKING INTO THE HOUSE, Natalie was surprised there was nobody in the office or the kitchen. It was a Wednesday. Maybe they closed the office for the party. Once again, Natalie wondered why the party was the day before Della's birthday … or did Max say the wrong day yesterday?

Noise came from the other side of the house, so Sam led her toward the open double doors. Her breath caught at the sight of the large room with a few tables in the middle. The room took up around a third of the main floor. The woodwork and polished floor gleamed in the sunlight streaming in through the windows.

"Welcome to the ball room." Max pointed at some chairs for them to sit in.

"It's beautiful." Sam took a seat beside her.

"It is. We rarely use it, but we have a party every now and again, so we have a reason to come in here." Max handed out beers.

Zachary was at the table with them, looking at Natalie closely. Too closely. He tipped his beer and asked, "How tall are you?"

"5'11," she answered, then tipped her beer at him.

"Did you play sports?" Zachary asked, his eyes scanning the room and watching those who were holding his kids.

"Yes, any I could," Natalie admitted. She was used to the question. It seemed once you were so tall everyone assumed that you played sports. When she was playing them, it hadn't bothered her at all, but now it was a bit annoying.

"Basketball?" he asked as the women came back into the room, and he refocused his attention solely on his wife.

"Yes, and volleyball and track. In fact, she was being recruited by colleges when she stopped playing." Sam jumped into the conversation as if he knew she was getting uncomfortable.

"You just quit?" he asked as his wife sat down next to him, his arm instantly going to rest on her chair to subtly touch her shoulder. Zephyr, for her part, leaned toward him.

Tearing her eyes from the intimacy of the couple, she told him, "No, I had a car accident and stopped playing. I just don't move like I used to."

"But she was good, which is why I was going to see if I could get her a coaching job this school year."

In all the days they had been together, he hadn't said anything, and before that, they hadn't spoken in years. When had he come up with this plan? And more importantly, why was he asking her in front of all these strangers?

"What?" Turning to him, she frowned at him bringing this up.

"You're good with kids. I even think the library would let you off to coach." He only smiled and took her hand in his.

"What sport?" she asked him. She had no experience coaching anything.

Her mind was instantly working, trying to solve how she would get out of work to coach. He was right, the library wasn't busy, so they would let her off. Especially since the library was so closely tied to the school. But what about the rest of her life? Did she even have time for this?

Shrugging, he admitted, "Volleyball. We're short a coach since Miller retired."

It was a sport she hadn't played since the accident—not that she had played any sports since that day. Questions ran through her mind about how she was supposed to coach when she couldn't play anymore. How was she supposed to coach when she didn't know how to? And why wasn't she instantly saying no? Why was she even thinking about it?

"Sam's a high school teacher." Max filled in the group watching the couple's discussion.

It was only then that she realized the room was quiet, and everyone was watching them. Being the center of attention had lost its luster over the years. That they were being watched made her blush and whisper to Sam, "I think we can discuss this later, Sam."

At her reaction, there were a few chuckles from the group as conversations started again. Natalie was silent as Sam and Zachary started talking about professional baseball. She wasn't interested in that sport; her mind was on when the last time she had even thought about volleyball. Without a doubt, she knew it had been years.

"Beckett," Zoe said in way of getting her attention, her elbows on the table and her head in her hands as she looked right at her. "How did you and Sam meet?"

"Sam was my history teacher during senior year. I made his life hell." Turning to the woman, Natalie tried to see if there was any resemblance between Zoe and herself, but she came up empty. There was nothing.

"Really? Isn't that against the rules? That has to be against school rules," Evie piped in from the next table over. It seemed she was paying attention to the conversation.

"It would have been, but we've only been a couple for a little while. Not while she was my student. That's just when we met," Sam informed them, his baseball talk was over, it seemed.

"Rules didn't really apply to me back then, or so I thought." Images floated through her mind of her senior year—what she had of it, at least.

When they finally got back to town, she hoped the people in Landstad wouldn't believe that anything had happened years before. There was no way she wanted Sam to get in trouble or be questioned about being inappropriate. With any luck, her being away from town for a long time and almost getting married would prove they were just what they seemed back then: teacher and student.

"Sounds like you, Zoe." Della's words surprised her. Though Zoe was by far the most outgoing of the siblings, she didn't seem to have the wild streak Natalie herself had.

"So, you were her teacher for just one year then?" Max asked Sam, the entire group now in on the conversation again.

"No, just fifty-one days." He surprised her with his answer.

Had he always known the day count? And he even removed the weekends from the count. Had he been counting? Had he always known?

The number surprised her, and she realized she had been in a coma longer than she had been a senior. More days had been spent sleeping than living life. Turning, she caught his eyes, and he smiled at her, and it warmed her that he knew the exact time.

"That's a steamy look. Must have been some great fifty-one days. Are you sure nothing happened back then?" one of the husbands asked. She couldn't remember their names.

"Not steamy then, just now. Back then, she was super annoying. Every one of them." Sam put his arm around her and pulled her closer for a kiss on the forehead.

"I did my best." She melted into his side, thinking about all the stuff she and the May kids got into—most of it he didn't even know. She knew her smile had faded with the memories.

"It's okay," he whispered in her ear. How he knew what she was thinking, she didn't know.

Glad when the conversation was overtaken by Zoe talking about her high school hijinks, Natalie was able to just listen. As the sisters talked about the past, she could tell they got along and spent a lot of time together. All except Zephyr, who didn't add a lot to the conversation about growing up.

As the conversation went on around them, Zephyr leaned toward her and asked, "How old are you? I can't really tell."

"Twenty-four," she lied. Her birthday was tomorrow, but it was close enough.

"Only three years younger than you are, Zephyr," Zachary said to his wife. Then said to Natalie, "Zephyr is the youngest of the sisters."

Zephyr smiled at her husband and said to Natalie, "You and I are closer in age than I am with Zoe, who is the next closest to me."

"You don't have the same memories as them? You're not joining in," Natalie said.

"I didn't grow up here. I was raised by our mother in Florida. They didn't know I existed until a few years ago. So I don't have as much in common like they all do." Zephyr looked over at the sisters, who were fighting over who someone was that had lived near them years ago.

All conversation stopped when Max got up and said that supper was ready. To Natalie's surprise, it was delivery pizza. Many, many of them. It was brought into the ballroom, and the kids came running down the stairs. The noise level in the room skyrocketed, and conversations were not possible.

The rest of the evening was spent in the ballroom talking about sports teams, new movies, actors, and people they knew. It was comforting to know that Zephyr was not involved in most of the conversations either. Sometimes she chatted with her husband or fussed over their kids, but she didn't feel the need to say something when she didn't want to. Natalie wanted to be more like Zephyr in her life—just let it go when possible. Let life happen around her without needing to join in.

Before the sun had set, Zachary announced that they would be going to the B&B for the night. With his words, Sam also stated that they should get going. Goodbyes were said with a round of hugs. Some even gave Sam and Natalie hugs. It was odd being included when she was wondering if she was even a part of the family. And if she was, they didn't know that.

As the other families headed to their cars, Zachary and Zephyr carried their kids across the road to the B&B, Sam and Natalie following behind. Once inside, Zachary remembered that he had forgotten to take out all their luggage from the car and headed back to get it. Sam went out to help him, carrying Zion.

Natalie sat down with Zephyr in the living room. "Zachary's very nice," Natalie said.

"That he is," Zephyr said, looking out the window at her husband opening the truck of the rental car.

"Can I hold her?" Natalie pointed at the baby.

After handing her off, Zephyr leaned back on the couch and asked, "Are you and Sam going to have kids?"

"Everybody keeps asking that." Natalie had the baby looking at her and answered the question at the baby. "No, Zephyr, we won't have any children. I can't have children."

"I'm sorry. I didn't realize." Zephyr's eyes went wide with regret.

"It's okay, I don't have a sign that says 'barren.' The car accident years ago affected me," she said in way of explaining.

"Are you wanting to adopt?" Zephyr asked as the men took a trip up the stairs with stuff.

"Yes, I want to adopt one day." But she wished that she could carry Sam's baby. Looking out the window, she saw Sam with Zion in his arms, and it melted her heart. She wanted any kid with that man—birth or adoption, it didn't matter.

"Zachary is adopted. And Della's girls are also adopted. She couldn't have children either," Zephyr said, watching Natalie with her baby.

"Did Max have an issue with it?" Natalie asked as Zephyr's words settled in. Had she been wrong this whole time and there was another Delphinea Hart out there that could have children?

"From what I heard, Max wanted Della, no matter what. You can see that when they're together. Della was the harder nut to crack; she didn't want him to settle for someone who couldn't have kids. But it worked out, as they got the girls just as they were getting married." Zephyr curled her feet under her.

"Max said tomorrow is her birthday, but the party was today?" Natalie took her shirt from the baby's mouth and replaced it with a toy her mother gave her.

"Her birthday is tomorrow. She doesn't celebrate it anymore. Max usually has a party around her birthday, but she spends the actual day alone. It's the one day she refuses to talk about. This year for her fortieth, us sisters are hoping to spend the day with her watching movies and such, letting her sulk with us if she lets us. If she kicks us out, I'll be around here if you guys want to do something."

Zachary indicated that he had everything in their room.

"Good luck." Natalie handed off the baby to Zephyr with a fake smile.

Watching her possible aunt walk up the stairs, Natalie was left wondering. Was this really her family? If this Della couldn't have children, where did that leave her? She had fallen in love with these people in the past two days, and now she was doubting that she even belonged. And if she did belong, Della didn't want her there.

Slowly, she walked up the stairs and into their bedroom. Sam was gone, so Natalie sat down on the bed and looked out the window into the back yard. She heard Sam come into the room, and he smelled like soap and toothpaste when he sat down next to her, but she didn't look at him.

"I made a mistake, Sam," she whispered as tears started to leak out of her eyes that she couldn't stop.

He put his arms around her and pulled her to him. "What mistake?"

"I don't think she's my mom. We don't look anything alike, and she can't have kids." She said her fears out loud and they sounded right.

"I think that she is, Natalie. You are so much like them, it's scary sometimes. They remind me a lot of you," he said into her hair.

"Even if she is, she doesn't like her birthday. She spends it alone. That was the day she had me. She didn't want me. Doesn't want me now. She doesn't want people to know about me." Why did she always have to cry? Why couldn't she be a little stronger?

"What do you want to do?" he asked.

"Leave," she whispered. "I can't stay here."

"I'll call my mom and see if we can stay at the cabin again. Tonight or tomorrow?" He pulled out his phone.

"Tonight. After Zephyr and Zachary are asleep. I can't say goodbye to them. I've no good explanation for it." Pulling out of his arms, she lay down on the bed and looked out the window.

Why did she even come here? What was she trying to prove? She could have just called the agency and gotten her real mom's phone number and address. Instead, she had guessed and had been so wrong. Now she didn't want another birth mom; she wanted this one. But this one wasn't her birth mom at all.

Or even worse, she was her mom and didn't want her. That she hadn't wanted her at birth and still didn't want her now. That Natalie's mere birth had made Della Hart's birthday intolerable. Even after twenty-four years.

Hearing Sam talking to his mom on the phone, she heard that the older couple had finally gone back to Fargo, and the cabin was empty. They could stay as long as they wanted. He hung up and changed clothes from his shorts that he slept in to jeans and a T-shirt. Then he packed both their suitcases, leaving her a sweatshirt out in case it got cold. All the while she sat, watching but not helping, unable to move as she cried.

Once he had everything packed, he asked if she was ready. She knew she would never be ready to leave the idea of being part of this family behind, but she had to. She didn't belong. Never would.

Sitting up, she wiped her face and got up, then dug through her bag and took out the disk her dad had given her to take for her mom. She set in on the dresser. If she was her mom, she should have the video, and if she wasn't, she could throw it away.

Looking at the video one last time, she traced the name her dad had printed on the label. 'Natalie's Life for Delphinea Hart.' Setting it down as Sam took her suitcase from her hand, she almost picked it up again to take it with her. This woman wouldn't want this, whether she was her real mom or not. But she walked away without it. Because it had been made for her.

CHAPTER 15

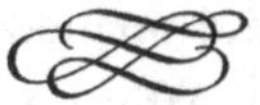

IT WAS FULLY DARK when they left the B&B with their suitcases after they were sure the other couple was sleeping. Natalie said nothing as they hit the road for his parent's cabin. Beside him, she was silent, and her emotions were raw. Holding her hand in the dark car, he wanted her to know he supported her. She was the most important thing to him.

Her tears had dried, though he knew they were still close to the surface. Whether it was right to leave or not, Natalie needed a break. The emotions from the moment she left her wedding until now had finally broken her, and she needed to get away from it all. Now she could start recovering from it.

He'd been relieved when he'd called his parents, and they said they had already left the cabin for home. If they were still there, he would have just gotten a hotel room for the night. He knew she didn't need his parents hovering around after today.

The drive went quickly, and she didn't say much during it. He knew that Della was the mother of Natalie Beckett. The girl herself might be doubting it, but he was not. Personality-wise, she had found her family, a family who would love to include her. Just look at her aunt, who was new to the family and still accepted for who she was.

But he was driving away from them all because Natalie had asked him to. And he would do anything for her. Because he had fallen in love with Natalie in just a few short days. He hoped that they could hold on to that love when they returned to their regular lives.

It was after midnight when they pulled up to his parent's dark cabin. At some point in the last fifteen minutes, she had fallen asleep. For most of the trip, she had been silent but awake.

Quietly, he took the bag and opened the cabin with the spare key his parents always had hidden. After putting their stuff in a bedroom, he went back to get her. He tried to pick her up and not wake her, but he failed when her green eyes opened, and she smiled at him. He didn't put her down, and she didn't ask to be put down. He just continued carrying her through the house to the bedroom that he had chosen and set her down on the bed.

"Do you want to share a room?" he asked a little too late. Maybe he was making assumptions since they weren't pretending to be a couple here. There were a lot of empty bedrooms, including the one she had slept in the last time they were there.

"Yes." She got up and went to the adjoining bathroom, taking her suitcase with her.

Sam stripped down to his boxers and waited on the bed for her to come out. When she finally did, she was surprisingly wearing only her panties. No shirt to cover the scars on her chest and stomach. He loved that she trusted him with her body. Walking straight to him, she cupped his face in her hands and said, "Thank you for everything you've done for me. You never even ask questions; you just do what I ask. I hope one day I can do the same for you."

Lowering her lips to his, she kissed him ever so lightly, once and then again. To his surprise, she climbed onto his lap and deepened the kiss.

His arms went around her and pulled her close to him.

The move made her moan into his mouth, and he quickly rolled her over to be on top. The move made her laugh. Her eyes sparkled at him as he said, "I have some ways in mind."

"I think I can read your mind, sexy Sam," she purred and ran her fingers down his back and grabbed his butt, pulling him closer to her.

Sam laughed until his mind emptied of any thoughts but her. Maybe she could read his mind because every move she made was perfect. Or maybe it was because she was just perfect for him.

CHAPTER 16

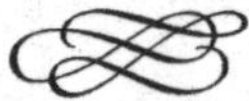

THE SUN WAS high in the sky over the lake that Sam's parents' cabin was on. They had been there since they had arrived in the middle of the night two days before, but today was the last day. They were heading out in the afternoon and going to Fargo and spending the night at his parent's house, then on to Landstad on Sunday. Sam was nice enough to make a stop in the middle of the trip to rest her back. But she had to get back to Landstad for book club since her honeymoon originally only went to Friday. Nobody knew how to run the podcast program, so she had to be there, no matter how much she wanted to stay here with Sam. There was no canceling book club.

They had spent her birthday mostly making love around the cabin and some in the water. She finally got to show him what she had planned for him when he thought she was drowning him, and it had worked. It also had the effect she had hoped for, and they had made love before getting back in the boat.

He hadn't given her a present for her birthday, but they hadn't been separated since he had rescued her from her wedding, so she forgave him.

To celebrate he had taken her out for supper in town. Over the course of the day, she had received texts and calls of birthday wishes, and she had actually responded to them all. The book club said that she better be home on time. She had a lot of explaining to do.

Friday was a rainy day, and they had spent it inside. They watched TV and talked about everything but the future. They had not broached that subject; they needed to get back to Landstad and be a normal couple before they could say whether this would work.

Now it was Saturday, a week since she'd ran out on her wedding. She could hardly believe it had only been one week. She was thankful she had Sam the entire time. What she would have done without him, she didn't know. And she was happy she didn't have to find out.

This Saturday, unlike the last one, turned out to be a hot and sunny day, no rain in sight. Sam had made a quick lunch, and they had eaten on the patio looking out at the water. When Sam had come out with a deck of cards, she knew they were in for an exciting afternoon. Maybe they should play strip poker? But not on the deck.

Smiling, she took the cards and started shuffling them. He sat down, and she started dealing. With an eyebrow raised, he asked, "What game do you want to play?"

"Strip poker." She gave him a sly grin.

"Anything you want, babe. I would love to see that body again when you lose." Leaning down, he kissed her and asked seriously, "Are you happy?"

"Yes. I haven't even cried in the last two days. A record for last week." She looked at the cards in her hand.

"It's only been a week?" he replied in awe and put his cards down.

"I bet you didn't get me a present for that either." She smirked at him.

He looked out at the water. "I might have something up my sleeve."

She turned to the water also and smiled. "Again, Sam? Don't you think the fish have seen enough of your backside."

She turned back to him a few seconds later, still smiling at the memory, but he was gone. Looking over at the patio door to see if he was there, she saw someone else. Della Hart was standing there, looking at her. Seeing the woman on the deck in gray slacks and a navy blue dress shirt and heels almost made Natalie laugh. The woman was dressed for the office, not for being in the hot sun by the lake.

She put her cards down on the table, upside down like you're supposed to so no one can see your hand as if she and Sam were going to continue playing.

"Can we talk, Natalie?" She said her name. After all the time they spent together, it sounded foreign coming from her.

"Yes, come and sit down." Natalie gestured to Sam's chair. Then she started to pick up the cards she had just dealt to put away, needing something to do with her hands.

"Can I hug you first? I've waited so long to hug you again," Della asked, walking to her.

Stopping what she was doing, she stood up and let the smaller woman hug her. After a moment, Natalie hugged her back. It was weird to be so much taller than her own mom, even her mom in high heels. Della pulled away and wiped a tear away as she sat down in the chair she had been offered.

"Did you watch the movie?" Natalie didn't know what else to say as she started to clumsily pick up the remaining cards.

"Yes. Over and over again. It was the best birthday present I've ever gotten. I had my daughter back. I called your dad, Patrick, and we talked. Mostly about you. I thanked him for being the best dad ever, all he did for you and mostly alone."

"He was great. I never lacked love in my life. Or support. My childhood was so perfect because of him." Natalie felt the tears coming again. Her dad had been her rock for her entire life. Yet she hadn't treated him as such all the time.

"Why didn't you tell me who you were?" Della asked, stopping her hands on the cards with her own, clasping them both in hers.

"I didn't know if you wanted to know me. I didn't know if I wanted to know you. I had great parents." The truth was easy to say.

"Why now? I got your letter years ago. I sent another, but I never heard from you again."

"I guess now my life was spiraling. Maybe not out of control, but it got emotional. A week ago today I was getting married. Not to Sam," she emphasized. "It was a guy I had dated for a few years, but we were comfortable, not in love. It doesn't matter now. But before the wedding, I stood in the basement of the church and wanted my mom there. That had never happened before. I had always had my dad. He was already enough. I knew that Lara was there, even if she had passed years ago. Dad always says she's there, and I knew she wouldn't miss my wedding. But I knew it was you I wanted there. I wanted my real mom to watch me get married."

"I would have loved to be there. If you had asked, nothing would have stopped me from being there." Della bit her lip, but it didn't stop them from trembling.

Sam walked quietly out of the house and put a tissue box between them.

"It wasn't only you. It was a lot of things. I made my friend Mia make sure that my friend Hazel was there, and she was. But I suddenly wanted her as a bridesmaid; I needed her as a bridesmaid. I suddenly felt that I couldn't get married without her as a brides-maid. I needed her as my friend again. I know what I'm saying makes no sense, and it makes no sense to me either, but that was what was running through my head then. So, I ran, literally, right into Sam's arms. He took me home and saved me again." She chuckled through her tears. "I asked him to take me to see you. I thought I could take care of that emotion first, the easier one. I have to go back and see Hazel and try and get over that emotion. That will be much harder."

"Hazel is the remaining triplet?" Della squeezed her hand.

Of course, Della would know about the triplets. They were a major part of her life—for twelve years, they were nearly the center of it. Their faces must have been in every frame of the videos. And she knew he would somehow have explained the accident aftermath.

Natalie just nodded. "I don't want to talk about it. It tends to send me into a depression."

"I'll not push you to open up to me. I'll not push you into anything you're not ready for. Why did you leave in the night?" She squeezed Natalie's hand.

"Are you mad I left?" Natalie asked, hoping the older woman would be able to forgive her.

"Hart's push away. It's what we do. Why did you run?"

"I just let my demons take over, let all the doubts get to me. I don't look like you. I really don't look like you." Natalie leaned back in her chair, letting her mom's hands go.

"I know. I knew you wouldn't. When I saw you at birth, I knew you would never look like me. You were dark-haired. Oh, so much hair. And even then, you were big, almost ten pounds. But I loved you right from the beginning." Della was looking at her, maybe comparing her to the baby of her memory.

"Why did you give me up?" Natalie needed to know.

"Because I was sixteen, and my father wasn't going to help. He wasn't like your father. I didn't think I had a choice." Della was starting to straighten the cards on the table between them.

"How about my father?"

"I don't know who it was." Della looked at the cards as she spoke, not at her daughter. "I went to a party at a fraternity at the university and drank too much. I woke up hours later and never knew what happened. I knew I'd had sex. That I could tell. Months later, I realized that I was pregnant. My dad was not happy."

"What were you doing at a college party at fifteen?" Natalie didn't even go to parties at fifteen. Okay, maybe she did, but not college parties.

"I was a college freshman, and my roommates got me to go." Della grinned at her and explained, "I skipped a few grades to get through school sooner."

Natalie wanted to know everything and nothing at the same time. "Did you get to pick who got me?" Had she known who her parents had been the entire time?

"No, that was all taken care of for me," Della admitted. "I don't know who made that decision. I was never even told."

"Did you ever want more kids of your own?" Natalie asked.

"Yes and no. Yes, I always wanted more kids. But no because I knew I was never going to have any. You were big, and it was a difficult delivery. I had an emergency hysterectomy the day you were born."

"I'm sorry." Natalie's heart broke for the girl her mother had been.

"It wasn't your fault. It was nobody's fault," Della assured her.

"They kept the name you gave me," Natalie said, though she knew Della knew her name was Natalie.

"I was happy when I saw that. They even had Hart as your middle name. I didn't give you one of those." Della smiled as she wiped her tears away.

"They loved Natalie because it meant Christmas, and they thought they were getting the best gift ever. My mom loved the Hart middle name and called me Natalie Hart all the time until she died. She thought it was like an endearment. Sometimes Dad uses it, too."

"Most of our spouses use it as an endearment also," Della said, looking out at the water. Then she asked, "Why did you have doubts that I was your mother?"

"I was talking to Zephyr, and she said you couldn't have children. I figured I made a mistake, and it wasn't you. I mean, look at me. Nothing like you at all."

"Poor Zephyr. She thought she had said something wrong when we realized you were gone."

"Don't get mad at her, please." Natalie didn't want to get between the sisters.

"I can never be mad at Zephyr. She's Zephyr. We didn't even know about her until a few years ago when she showed up like you, but we weren't looking for her. She was raised in foster care and has a hard time in groups. And our family does things as groups."

"So, she knew about you? But you didn't know about her?" Natalie asked.

"Yes. Zephyr knows why I can't have children, but she didn't put the two together. I should have told her it was you. I just thought I had time. Our birthdays." Della looked out at the lake.

"You knew?" Natalie looked closely at her.

"Yes, almost right away. You act so much like Zoe, and you have my eyes. I had my doubts because you didn't look like the picture I had of you, but then you said you had an accident. You've had facial work?" Della touched her own face.

"Yes, reconstructed cheekbone and jaw, so it changed how I look. The accident was bad." Natalie didn't go into any more details. She knew her father had gone over a few in the video. There was no way he could have skipped over it. It was so much a part of her life for so long.

"I wanted you to tell me. I just should have said it, but I was a little scared that I was wrong. I wanted her to be you." Della held a tissue to her eyes again.

Natalie held out her hand. "I wanted my mom to be you too."

Della put her hand in her daughter's and asked, "Can I be a part of your life? Even just a small part? I know you have your dad, and he is your parent. I'm not asking to be a mom, but a friend. Family? Just something."

"I hope you can. I do live far away, about five hours or so. That's a long way."

"I can drive that. I would drive anywhere to see you—even for just a moment. And there's always room at the B&B for you and Sam. And there's a family discount." She smiled at her. "It's no charge."

"Sam and I are working out if we *are* a we right now."

"You really looked in love, Natalie."

"We might be, but it's been a roller coaster this week. We have to get back to Landstad and see if we can take on the mundane life stuff," Natalie admitted in fear.

"If you can handle the emotional stuff, the mundane is easy after the roller coaster," Della replied.

"We have a couple of things to get over first: I was supposed to be married now, and he was my teacher once," Natalie pointed out.

"That's nothing big. You're still wearing his ring." Della pointed to Natalie's hand.

She hadn't taken the ring off since Sam had placed it on her hand on Tuesday. Without it, she thought her hand would look naked, feel naked. And that maybe the magic would wear off, and Sam wouldn't be the man she had fallen in love with. "I think we just need to get back among people who know us both. My dad is all for it, but what if everyone else thinks it's weird?"

"They won't," Della assured her. "And even if they do, it doesn't matter. Not if you love him."

CHAPTER 17

THEY ENDED up getting a late start at leaving. But Sam loved that Natalie had been able to have supper with her mom. The couple had not brought their girls on the trip, so it had been just the four of them. Della told them stories about growing up and when she had come back to town to start a law practice. Max was always quick with a comment but willing to let his wife do most of the talking. Which was perfect because it was Della that Natalie was most interested in.

Natalie told them about many of the events from her childhood and teen years. Many of the stories she told he had never heard before. Not all showed her in the greatest light upon retelling, but Natalie told them anyway. He wondered how much was in the video that she had left, but knowing Patrick, it was long and detailed.

He noticed that as she got to her later teen years and beyond, the stories were shorter, and there were far fewer. She had even skipped over the accident and the year following completely. If the older couple realized it, they didn't comment.

As he locked his parents' cabin, he watched her hug her mom, with Della holding on a little longer with each hug the two exchanged. From a distance, they were opposites, but Sam could tell they were related by the little things: hand motions and actions that neither of them probably noticed.

He had been a little nervous that Natalie would be mad at him for inviting them over, especially without asking her. When Patrick had called him and said that Della wanted to see her, to explain, Sam knew Natalie needed to hear what the woman had to say. Whether it was that she wanted a relationship with Natalie or not, Natalie needed to hear it from the woman herself. It had been his idea for the surprise visit, feeling it would be easier on her nerves. She had a tendency to overthink things and jump to the wrong conclusion.

After the hug and then another for the road, he loaded Natalie into the car to head west and then north the next day. With promises to call soon, the cars headed out in opposite directions. After a few miles of Natalie sitting in silence, he wanted her to not get lost in the emotions. "Feeling better now?"

"Yes. I should have stayed in Birch Cove." She admitted.

"You went with your gut. It was maybe better this way. You got some one-on-one time with her. That might not have happened in Birch Cove with all your aunts around."

His words made her smile because suddenly she had aunts. She had a big family. "You might be right. One day I want to go back and really meet them all. Even Zephyr." She looked out the window.

Sam wondered if the two women had a connection being so close in age. Della had informed them that Zephyr was an author Natalie was a fan of but Sam had never heard of. Natalie had been excited about the idea she was related to the woman, even if she couldn't tell anyone because Zephyr preferred that people didn't know. "I hope we can get back also. They're nice people." He looked at the road.

"Yes, they are." She looked at the road ahead of them. "I think she helped me with some of the accident stuff."

"I didn't think you even talked about it." He was surprised.

"We didn't. She told me about giving me up and not wanting to, but she couldn't stop it from happening. It was like it had to happen. Like the accident—it happened, and I couldn't stop it. I still can't stop it. It happened, and I just have to learn to live with that." Natalie sighed.

"Can you live with it?" he asked.

"I won't know until I talk to Hazel. I want us both to get past it. I know we both still have a lot of issues because of it."

He liked that she wanted to include Hazel in her journey of healing. He hoped the other woman was willing to walk it. Grabbing her hand, he held it before asking, "How about us? Are you nervous to get back?

"Yes and no. I don't want to be talked about, but I want to get back to a normal life and make sure you still like me when I forget to do laundry. I hate laundry." Smiling at him, she squeezed his hand.

"I don't think that will be an issue—the laundry part. I think it'll take a week for you to decide you want to move in with me." He took her hand in his. She was still wearing his ring, and he didn't ask her about it. He wanted her to wear it, to be his.

"Confidence, Sullivan." She giggled.

"I have confidence in us, Natalie." He kissed the back of her hand, loving that she was happy, relaxed. So different from what she had been just days before when they had traveled this road the other way.

As the miles went by, silence filled the car once more. Should he have said that about them? Was he being pushy about them being a couple? It had only been a week since he took her home from her wedding. Was he being overconfident in the relationship? It had been years since he was even in a long-term relationship. Why was he so sure this one was the one that was going to make it? What was it about Natalie that made him sure they were going to make it?

But no matter how much or how little time he had known her, he was sure she was the one. When he realized it, he didn't know. It had been slow coming over the week, just little things here and there. But in total, he was in love with her. Every bit of her.

Glancing over, he saw she was looking at her phone. Her black hair was pinned up in a loose bun today, leaving her neck exposed. He had kissed that neck already today, many times, but wanted to do it again.

The hours slipped by easily as they made small talk, and soon, they were pulling into his parents' driveway. His mother had assured him it was okay that they stayed with them overnight. He wondered if she would pull out picture books again and ask if they needed separate bedrooms. This time they would not.

Sue Sullivan rushed out when the car stopped and ushered Natalie into the house, leaving Sam to get the luggage. There was no doubt who the guest of honor was today. While walking through the house, his mother directed him to bring them to the guest bedroom then join them in the living room. Entering the room, he set her bag on the bed and turned to leave. But his father was blocking him from leaving.

"You both can stay in this room if you want." Steve nodded at his suitcase.

"You have never let one of us boys stay with a girl in their room, Dad." Though he wanted to spend the night with her, he wasn't sure she would be comfortable with that at his parents' house. When they were there.

"But this one is the one, Sam," his dad assured him.

"So was Isla, and Seth still had to sleep on the couch two summers at the cabin, even after they were engaged. You two are getting crazy in your old age." Sam laughed and dropped his suitcase on the bed.

"Isla wasn't going anywhere, Sam. Natalie … You need to work at not losing her. Your mom wants more grandbabies."

Stiffening, he looked at his dad. "There won't be grandbabies with this one, Dad."

"Grandbabies come in many forms, Sam." His dad surprised him with his answer. His parents had never said anything about adoption, not once in his life.

"I know," he agreed. It hadn't taken him long to get used to the idea of adoption, not when he was adopting with Natalie.

"Do you love her?" His dad leaned against the door jam.

"Yes. But she's a little hesitant about it."

"Well, she almost got married last week, that takes time. You have to remember you have had feelings for her for years—she hasn't had that." His dad wasn't done with his little lecture, it seemed, because he wasn't moving.

"I haven't had feelings for years," Sam protested.

"Really? I think you were half in love with her when she almost died in your arms. You talked about her before, and I thought she was special to you then as well. That was why the accident affected you so much. The ones who died you didn't talk about, but you always talked about her."

"She was the one I tried to help. The only one alive," Sam argued. He had been there, not his dad. If he could have saved them all, he would have. They were all important to him; they were all someone worth saving. That the survivor had been Natalie and that he had fallen for her had been a coincidence.

Or had it? He couldn't see himself thinking about sharing a bedroom with Hanna May. No matter how many years it had been, Hanna was still a student in his mind. And it wasn't because she died, because he always thought of her sister Hazel as a student also. Natalie had been different from the beginning.

Steven had been watching him and said, "She's the one you couldn't let go of. She was important to you then too."

He couldn't find a response as Steve nodded his head as he turned and walked away, leaving Sam confused about his feelings or when they had started. Sam slumped on the bed between the suitcases, forgetting about saving Natalie from his parents downstairs. Had he liked her back then? If he was being truthful, he did. He remembered waiting for senior history all day. Remembered his eyes would always find her in the hallway between classes. Going to volleyball games just to see her play. He would even sit by Patrick to watch, and at one, Patrick had let him record the game.

Sighing, he realized he should have been fired for lusting after a student. But no other woman or girl had ever affected him like that. Just Natalie Beckett. Holding her dying body had just complicated everything, but maybe that made it deeper than it would have been if the accident had not happened. What if this wasn't love like he thought? Maybe it was just some odd attraction from his past coming to the surface.

Natalie suddenly rushed into the room, closed the door behind her, and leaned on it. "Your mom is making pancakes for breakfast. And I think she's going to start talking about wedding colors. She hinted about it. I think your parents are moving too fast for me. The pressure is suffocating."

Pushing his thoughts away, he faked a smile and said, "I know they're moving too fast. Because they wanted us married a week ago."

"Oh, I can tell." She stood straight again and walked over to him. Taking his face in her hands, she asked, "What's the matter? You're sad."

He loved and hated how she could read him. "Just thinking about the past."

"The accident?"

He hated that she knew he was haunted by it also. "Kind of. Dad said he thinks I liked you before the accident. Inappropriately." He watched her green eyes for shock. None came.

Smiling, she kissed his lips lightly. "I liked you inappropriately from the first day I saw you."

"Natalie, I'm serious. I was your teacher." Sometimes he hated how flippant she could be.

"Sam, Sam, Sam. I had the biggest crush on you in high school. It was the reason I teased you all the time. It was the reason I got in trouble all the time, just to get your attention. It was the reason I couldn't go all the way with Henry. And it was the reason I called you sexy Sam all the time—because you were so damn sexy. But nothing, absolutely nothing you did was inappropriate. It was all me." Still holding his face in her hands, she kissed his cheek.

"I was your teacher. It would have been the end of my career," he whispered as she kissed across his nose and to his other cheek.

"Except nothing happened, Sam. You would have never let anything happen. I think the accident was good for us. It separated us until we were old enough to do it right. Now we're going to do it right." She kissed his mouth and didn't let him talk for a long time.

CHAPTER 18

Natalie glanced at the clock on the dash as they pulled into Landstad late Sunday afternoon, far later than she had planned. She had hoped to talk to her dad today, but she was already almost late for book club. After book club, she couldn't talk to him since she would probably be drunk. It was always a bad idea to have a heart-to-heart while drunk—way too much heart showed up.

There was always drinking at book club, that was how they could keep talking for hours. And tonight, she had to tell everyone about Sam and her. And explain the wedding and the week. It was going to be a long one.

"Do you just want me to drop you off downtown?" he asked as they neared Ruth's downtown apartment. Since it was a small town, he knew where she lived. Actually, he knew where almost everyone lived. And he knew that was where book club was always held.

When they had started, Ruth had lived alone and had a great apartment big enough for the six of them with no issues. Not that she had moved, but now she lived with her boyfriend Anderson, and she had better snacks. Anderson was far better of a cook than Ruth. Now every other weekend, he would find something else to do for the afternoon of book club, leaving the girls to his apartment.

"No, I have to grab the stuff from home first." At this point, she was still carrying all the podcast equipment back and forth every two weeks, not wanting to bother Ruth about storing the stuff, even if Natalie knew she had room—she owned the entire building after all. But since she edited it before putting it online, she had to have most of the equipment with her anyway, so she kept it all.

"How much stuff do you need for a book club?" he questioned, not for the first time since she said she needed to drive herself.

Smiling and biting her lip, she knew she couldn't tell him the truth about book club. Nobody in the group wanted anyone in town to know that they recorded a podcast, so kept it under wraps to almost everyone. She wasn't ready for Sam to know yet. And she had no time even if she did, she was late. "More than you think," was all she said as he pulled up to her dad's house. It looked quiet today. "Looks like no one is home."

"Looks that way." He got out of the car also, casually looking around. Natalie wondered if he was looking for Jason to jump from the bushes or her dad.

Jumping out of the car, she gathered her things from the front seat while he grabbed her suitcase from the back. Together they walked into the empty house. A note on the table said her dad was off at Faith's place for the evening. Sam followed her to her bedroom. She knew she should say something, but she didn't know what to say. They were back, and things had already changed.

"When can I see you, Natalie?" He put the suitcase down on her bed.

"I don't know," she replied, unable to look into his eyes.

"Are you not even going to give this a chance now that we're back?" He sounded exasperated.

"It's not that. It's just tonight is book club, and tomorrow I have to work," she explained. Her life was busy, and being gone for a week had made it worse.

"Tomorrow night?" He was beginning to sound angry.

"I have to talk to my dad. A long talk. About everything. I promised him before I left." Natalie wished she could put off her talk with him, but her dad deserved to hear about her trip. Actually, he deserved so much more, but a meal and a talk were what he was getting.

"Tuesday?" Sam folded his arms. Now he was angry.

"Yes, but I'll call you if something happens." She turned to grab her computer bag and the box of equipment, glad she had a box with a cover on it. There would be too many questions if he could see in the box.

"In case you get too busy?" Taking the box from her, his look dared her to take it back.

"No, Sam, in case I can get away sooner. Quit being mad at me. I don't know how to do this." She left the room.

Silently, he followed her to her car in the driveway. She watched him put the box in the back seat as she opened the driver's door. Tossing the bag across the car to the passenger seat, she turned to him. He was leaning against the car, watching her. "Sam, I really want to see if what we had last week will be the same here."

His arms went around her, and he nuzzled her neck. "Me too, Beckett."

His lips on her neck made her laugh as she pushed him away. "I have to go, I'm already late. And I have all the equipment." She cringed at her words since there shouldn't be equipment for a book club. Before she climbed into the car, she pulled him to her and kissed him, but unfortunately, he kissed her back, and she was even later getting on the road. Her heart was racing, and her body was all tingly as she drove the six blocks to downtown.

As she parked her car, she saw Hazel's Beetle and Tess's sporty red SUV were already there. Mia and Mandy lived just across the street, so they were probably there. Natalie was last and late. Getting all her stuff together, she climbed the stairs to Ruth and Anderson's apartment. Sometimes she wished she could live downtown with Ruth, Mandy, and Mia. Not long before, Tess lived there as well, but she had moved in with her boyfriend recently.

At the top of the stairs, she chose to knock on the door because she was tired of opening and closing doors while balancing the heavy box.

Maybe she should leave the headphones and soundbox at Ruth's. It was annoying to carry back and forth. And who knows where she'd be living in two weeks. She knew where she wanted to be, but it just seemed too soon. Then there would be so much talk.

Ruth opened the door and grabbed the box right from her arms. Following Ruth into the apartment, she saw the other four women were at the table with drinks in front of them, and nobody was talking anymore. All eyes were on her.

"Hi, everyone. Sorry I'm late. Sam would not speed no matter what I said." She headed to the couch to unload her computer like every other week, hating being the center of attention.

"Sam, is it?" Tess smirked from the table.

"You can take your time with the computer, Nat. You have some explaining to do before we can start anything." Mia smirked from behind her glass of whiskey.

Natalie shot her a look. Had she told everyone what she knew or kept it a secret? Just now realizing that though she didn't want everyone to know she was adopted, she wanted to tell everyone about meeting her mom. About the new family she had found.

"I thought we would do the podcast first, then talk. Like always." Natalie pulled out the computer, trying to stall as she opened it and turned it on.

"That was before you left us all at your wedding." Ruth sat back in the chair at the head of the table she had left to open the door.

Natalie sat down, put her hands over her closed computer, and looked at the group. They were her closest friends, from Hazel with her blonde pixie cut to Mia whose hair was still brown from the wedding, something Natalie had been sure she would change the day, and the three blonds between them. "What do you want to know?"

"Are you married?" Tess was the first with a question, probably because she was the only one who wasn't drinking, thanks to her pregnancy.

"No, why? You were at the wedding. It didn't happen." Natalie got up to get a drink from the counter, feeling the pressure of the eyes on her.

"Then why do you have a wedding ring on?" Tess pointed out, holding up her hand and wiggling her own fingers. Four sets of eyes went to the hand holding the mixed drink she had just poured.

She, too, looked at the ring. She hadn't taken it off and had forgotten she still wore it. Sitting down, she said, "Sam and I faked a marriage."

"Why?" Ruth asked, grabbing her hand to analyze the ring.

"We stayed at a bed-and-breakfast."

"I don't think you have to fake a marriage for that. They didn't check, did they? I mean, are there rules about marriage before staying at a bed-and-breakfast?" Mandy asked in confusion as she leaned back in her chair.

"I needed to disguise my name. I couldn't be Natalie, so I became Beckett Sullivan."

"I like it, can I use it?" Ruth said. She was a romance author. Natalie didn't know if it was the story or the name that she wanted to use, but it didn't matter.

"Why, Natalie?" Tess pushed her friend's shoulder for asking her question since it really didn't explain anything.

Looking around at the faces at the table, Natalie took a deep breath and said, "Because I was going to see my mother. I didn't want her to know it was me."

Hazel gasped, and her hand went over her mouth. "Natalie, your mom is dead." Eyes wide at the statement, she tried to say something else, but the words didn't seem to come out.

Turning to her, Natalie touched her arm in comfort. "Haze, I'm adopted. I went to see my birth mom."

The fact had never crossed her mind as she grew up, enough so that she had never told her best friends. Even Hanna had never known, and Hanna had known nearly everything about her.

"I never knew," Hazel finally said, looking her up and down. "But it makes sense."

"That's what I said," Mia spoke for the first time.

Smiling at her, Natalie realized she hadn't given up her secrets while she was gone. But now that word was out, she could say what she had wanted to all the while.

"Did you get to meet her?" Ruth asked, leaning on the table toward Natalie with interest.

"Yes. We talked about everything. I know way more about me than I used to." Natalie looked around the room and noticed everyone was listening and nobody was drinking.

"Does she look like you?" Hazel asked.

"No, she's a short redhead. I take after my father." It sounded wrong to call the man she would never know her father when she had a father whom she loved and couldn't see her life without. In the future, she would have to come up with a different name for the man who she was not interested in knowing. Not just because replacing her dad wasn't an option, but because he didn't even know she existed and shouldn't due to how she was conceived.

"What does he look like?" Mia asked.

"Me, I assume, but she doesn't know his name or anything," Natalie told her friends, not telling them what her mom had said.

"Are you going to see her again?" Tess asked.

"Yes, we'll keep in contact, and if I ever get married again, she'll come. And probably bring a slew of relatives." She couldn't stop the smile on her face—she had relatives.

"If you get married? Are you going to turn the fake marriage into a real one?" Mandy pointed at her finger and teased. "You know, so you can stay at a bed-and-breakfast again."

"Maybe, one day," she admitted to the group.

"How did the Sam thing happen?" Ruth asked.

"He picked me up in the parking lot. Literally. And took me to his place. I stayed there for a few days, then we went on the trip," Natalie explained to the group, not going into too much detail. They didn't need to know about how nice he had been or how he had comforted her. That was for her to know.

"He lives behind her dad. Their backyards touch," Mia explained with two index fingers touching in front of her face, letting everyone know she had the inside scoop. That she had known but hadn't been telling them.

"Convenient." Tess sipped her lemon water, then frowned at it. Tess was not loving the no alcohol part of pregnancy and usually talked about it during their get-togethers.

"We'll see," Natalie said. "But before that, Ruth, do you have a place for me to rent?"

Ruth choked on her mixed drink at the question. "I'll have to check." Ruth happened to own most of the buildings downtown and rented out the apartments above the businesses. Though it was a new development—that people knew, not that she owned them. She had owned them for years.

"Why not just move in with sexy Sam?" Mia grinned with a wink.

"Why move out of your dad's place?" Hazel asked in seriousness.

Ignoring Mia, Natalie turned to Hazel and said, "My dad is probably going to move his girlfriend and her kids in. They don't need me around too."

"When did this happen? A girlfriend? I thought that one day Mrs. Champ would finally make a move. Poor Mrs. Champ." Hazel took a long drink of her mixed drink.

Natalie grinned at Hazel calling the woman Mrs. Champ still, but to her, Faith was just her art teacher. That had been how Natalie had seen her until recently. Now she was Faith, her dad's girlfriend. "There's no poor Mrs. Champ—she nabbed him years ago. He's just been dragging his feet. But not anymore. He tried to tell me it was because he didn't know how I would react, but I'm so happy for him. And would have been years ago." Natalie opened her computer and turned it on.

"Why don't you just move in with Sam?" Mia asked again, not liking being ignored.

Turning to her, Natalie said, "Because we're taking it slowly, Mia. We don't want people to talk."

"People will talk anyway. Whether it's tomorrow or in three years, people will talk. Just let them and live your life. I like to have something to talk about; it makes my days go faster," Mia said with a giggle.

"I don't need them talking to me about it," Natalie admitted.

"They won't talk to you about it? They will talk to me and everyone else about it. Do you want me to tell people that you've been having a steamy affair for months? I can make it happen." Mia finished her glass of whiskey and set it loudly on the table, causing a frown from Ruth.

"No, Sam doesn't need people talking like he stole me or we had an indecent affair. He's a teacher," Natalie reminded the group.

"Indecent." Tess laughed at the word.

"Improper," Mia agreed and giggled.

"Obscene." Mandy tried to keep a straight face before snorting.

"Risqué," Hazel joined in.

"Dirty." Mia laughed.

"Saucy." Ruth couldn't contain herself.

All five were laughing as Natalie rolled her eyes at them and clicked through to the program she was looking for. Ignoring them, she got up and handed out the headphones. Each took a pair and adjusted them as they laughed and added a few more choice words about her so-called affair.

"Very funny. We have to get started, or you guys will all be passed out before we get halfway done, and it'll be Tess and me chatting away as the only sober ones in the room." Natalie sat down and made sure they all had their headphones on.

CHAPTER 19

To her surprise, the recording went smoother than they usually did, and nobody actually got too drunk. Usually, she limited them to two drinks for the recording because if they had too many, they'd get off topic but too few, and they were not as funny.

Pressing stop on her computer, she pulled off the headset and watched the others do the same. She turned her attention to closing her computer programs, letting the conversation go on around her. They were still arguing about who had to read the worst book on John Wayne Gacy. Early on, they decided that they would all read different books and compare them while telling the story of the killer. It had worked out great because they all came in with a different perspective.

Closing the computer, she glanced up to see Hazel looking at her. Smiling at her friend, she asked quietly so not to get everyone else's attention, "How are you, Haze?"

"Okay. And you?"

"I'm getting better, I think. I did a lot of thinking and remembering this week and the week before. I want to get together and talk about it. Try to get past it," Natalie said, and the rest of the group got quiet.

"Maybe, one day," Hazel agreed, not meeting her eyes as she looked at the ice that was all that remained of her drink, but Natalie knew she didn't mean it.

With that, the conversation died between them, and Mia started to talk about what happened while Natalie was gone. Mostly it was nothing, but a few interesting things were brewing in town. And, of course, Mia knew about it.

Half-listening, she watched to see that Hazel was only half-listening as well. Ruth was talking about the football team, who were doing pretty good this year, and Mia was saying that the volleyball team had no coach yet, so that was probably going to be dropped this year. Hazel's eyes bounced from Ruth to Mia to Mandy to Tess, but not to Natalie. Never to Natalie. Wishing she could make Hazel talk, she tried to catch her eye but couldn't.

The laughter and joking from before the recording were gone, at least for Hazel and Natalie. The others seemed not to have noticed. Natalie was deciding whether to have another drink or to just leave when she noticed Hazel leaving. Quickly, she finished the drink she had left and grabbed her computer.

Turning to Ruth, she asked, "Can I just leave the headphones here for the next few weeks? I don't want to have to move them around to wherever I land."

"Of course," Ruth agreed, coming over to her and putting the cover on the box that was staying with her. "I'll text you when I find out if I have a place."

"Thanks." Natalie slung the bag over her shoulder. "I should get going. I didn't even get to do anything when I got back. We were so late."

Everybody said goodbye as she walked out the door, waving at them. Down the stairs, she went and put her bag in her car slowly. Closing the door, she leaned against her car, knowing Hazel would have to walk past her to get to her own car. Natalie stared into the night sky as she waited for what seemed like a long time before Hazel came through the door of Ruth's apartment.

Natalie saw the moment Hazel noticed she was still there. Her steps slowed, and her back stiffened. She was probably debating just going back into the apartment or walking the other way. Anything but walking by Natalie.

"Hazel, I want to talk to you," Natalie said to her friend.

"I don't think we have anything to say to each other, Natalie." Hazel ran her hand through her short hair as she spoke, a nervous habit Natalie recalled from way back.

"But we do. We have everything to say. We never talk," Natalie argued.

"We don't need to talk," Hazel assured her, still not moving.

"It's like a black cloud hanging over us."

"It's all around us, Natalie, not hanging over us. It's everywhere," Hazel explained, and Natalie knew she was right. It was all around them, and they hadn't been able to find their way out. But Natalie was suddenly on the edge, and she wanted out.

"I want to get through it. I want you to get through it," she explained.

"I don't see me ever getting through it; it's been a lot of years, and it's still as fresh as it was the day it happened." Hazel shoved her fists into her front jean's pockets.

"How did you find out about the accident?" Natalie had started to take an interest in what happened after the accident when she was in a coma. Sam made her realize that the accident hadn't only affected those involved; it rippled to everyone. And those affected first had been affected the most.

"They woke me up to help identify the bodies. So, I saw them. Both of them," Hazel whispered.

Natalie knew how bad she had looked after the accident, and she knew the funerals had been closed casket. Sam had told her that. But Hazel had seen them. Her grandparents should have never made her do that when she was so young, and it angered Natalie that they had. She had been seventeen and still a kid.

"Why? Why did they do that?" she asked.

"I don't know, but I see them in my dreams like that. Always dead." Hazel's voice cracked.

"Hazel." Natalie went to take her friend in her arms, but Hazel backed away from her into a wall.

"No, Natalie, no. You can't make it better. Maybe you can get over it, but I never will. My life stopped that day. I was no longer who I had been, who I was going to be." Hazel's back was now against the brink wall.

"Hazel, you can't have that day decide your life," Natalie said, knowing that in some ways, she had let that day decide her life.

"Yes, I can. I think of it every day. I am here because I am all that is left."

"You shouldn't be here. You need to follow your dreams. You need to sing again," Natalie said to her friend whose talent was bigger than this town. Hazel wouldn't stop singing when they were growing up, but since coming back, Natalie hadn't heard her once.

"Over the last few years, I would sometimes go to Grand Forks to parties. Just college parties. There was a band that would let me sing during their breaks. I've quit that." Hazel ran a hand through her hair, messing it up completely.

"That sounds amazing, Hazel. Why quit?" Natalie was both shocked and intrigued by her admission. Seeing Hazel perform had always been a treat, seeing her perform at not a school function would have been amazing.

"Grandma didn't want to watch John Henry all the time," was all she answered.

"But you need time away from him," Natalie argued.

"No, I don't. He's my responsibility. Nothing is more important than him." Her voice was louder than it had been, and she was almost yelling at Natalie.

"Of course not, Hazel. That's not what I meant." Natalie moved toward her friend again, but again, Hazel backed away, her back sliding along the harsh brick wall to get away from her.

"I'm going to quit book club soon. She's complaining a lot about me being gone. She has to watch him all day when I'm in the fields. She doesn't want to watch him all night. I need to be there for my son." Hazel was trying not to cry as she spoke.

"You can bring him. You know you can. Nobody will say anything." The others would gladly have the boy at book club.

"Nobody else has a kid they would bring, and he's almost four. We cannot talk about murder in front of him. By winter, I'll stop, maybe sooner. Maybe I won't come next time," Hazel admitted.

"Hazel, you can't quit. You're important to the group." Natalie started to worry about her oldest friend. That more than the accident was affecting her, that living with the grandparents who raised her might be a bigger issue.

"No, Natalie, you won't notice me when I'm gone. You never did before." Her voice sounded small, even to Natalie.

"Yes, we will. We all love you."

Hazel let the comment slide, turned, and started for her car, then stopped. "Good luck with Mr. Sullivan. Without him, I wouldn't have graduated. I missed a lot of school, and he made sure my diploma was signed. He's a good guy, and you deserve a good guy."

Natalie watched her get into her little yellow car and drive away. Every time she talked to Hazel alone, it got worse and worse. Maybe because each time they talked, she got a little better, but Hazel didn't. Hazel maybe got a little worse.

Should she head back to Ruth's to talk to the group about Hazel wanting to quit? No, they could talk about that when everyone was sober. Maybe she would call a meeting about it. She knew that they would do everything they could to keep Hazel in the group. And maybe it would be better if she wasn't a part of it.

Getting into her car, she looked at the time: just past 8:00 p.m. The short drive home didn't give her enough time to figure anything out about Hazel or even Sam. Parking in the driveway, she realized that her dad had not returned home yet. The house was quiet and didn't feel like home like it always used to.

Going to her room, she started to unpack her bag, then thought better of it. Leaving it all packed, she grabbed her small bag of toiletries and an outfit for work in the morning, wrote a note to her dad, and headed out the back door. Running through the grassy back yard, she tried the back door to Sam's house. The door was unlocked, so she slipped inside, hoping he wouldn't get mad at her for breaking into his house.

Walking into the living room, she saw him on the couch watching TV, but he was sleeping. Quietly, she slipped past him and put her stuff in the bedroom, then went back to the living room. He was sitting up with his feet on the coffee table, head back on the back cushions, still sleeping.

Smiling, she left him and went to his bedroom, slipping out of her clothes. She took out her cell phone and called him.

"Hello," he answered, sounding groggy.

"Are you sleeping?" she smiled as she asked.

"No, just watching TV," he lied.

"Can I come over?" she asked as she slid out of her panties.

"Sure."

"I'll be over in a minute." She shut off her phone.

Putting the phone on the side table, she climbed onto the bed and waited, trying not to laugh out loud as she heard him run down the hallway toward the bedroom. Probably to change clothes.

He appeared in the doorway and abruptly stopped when he saw her. A smile overtook his face as he looked over her naked body in his bed.

"You lied to me. You were sleeping." She watched him take off his shirt on his way to the bed.

"You said you weren't here." He slid his shorts and underwear off and climbed into bed beside her.

"OK, I lied too," she said before his mouth claimed hers.

CHAPTER 20

IT HAD TAKEN A WEEK. Just one short week. By Saturday afternoon, two weeks after her aborted wedding, she was completely bored with life. The first few days of the week had been full—getting back to work and putting her life back in order—but then it quickly slid into boring.

She realized that before the wedding, every moment was spent planning. It had taken her a year to plan the thing, and every small detail had been organized to death. It had been a year of all-out focus on that one day. It had been beautiful, and everything had worked out as planned, except her actually getting married.

Before the year of wedding planning, she had been focused on school. Studying and writing papers occupied her time. Though the work had always been easy, she had always given 110% to everything after the accident. Papers were longer than they needed to be. Assignments were completed as soon as possible, and sometimes she did them twice. Books were read twice so she would know the information.

Now she had nothing to do. Nothing at all.

Monday morning, she had woken up in Sam's arms and was almost late for work. During her lunch that day, she had bitten the bullet and called Jason, explained that it wasn't him, it was all her. He was still mad, and nothing she said would change that. She understood and was happy that they didn't need to separate their things.

After spending the afternoon dwelling on it, going to her dad's that evening for supper had been exactly what she needed. It was just the two of them like old times, but to Natalie, everything had changed. Their lives had changed from their last meal.

Over grilled chicken, she told him about meeting her birth mom and Della's family. And about the story of where she came from. He needed to know. She told him about her stay with Sam and his parents at the cabin and alone at the cabin, leaving out some details. But since she hadn't slept at home the night before, he probably could fill in those details.

He told her about his and Faith's plans to actually move in together. The woman had jumped at the idea of combining their families after all this time. Patrick said that they were going to move into the house Natalie had been raised in since it was bigger, and Patrick already owned it. No wedding or engagement had been decided on. Try living together first, he had told her. But Natalie knew that it wouldn't take long for that to change—her dad was a great person to live with.

By the end of the conversation, Natalie felt that her personal life was in order. Her dad was happy and actually moving on with his life, and she was just as happy and moving on with her life. Both of them were going in a different direction than they had thought they would be going two weeks before.

After the meal, when she grabbed a few things from her room and headed over to Sam's for the night, Patrick said nothing. Smiling across the two yards, she knew she would not be moving into a place downtown. She would stay right here with Sam. Living behind Patrick, close enough to watch him as he started his new life, made her love him even more. Because he was the perfect dad.

Tuesday night, she had worked on the podcast alone in Sam's bedroom. He had tried to get out of her what she was doing, but she would not say: what happens at book club stays at book club. It had been the moto since the first day. It was why they were so open with each other.

Once edited and uploaded, she went to find Sam to take his mind off her ignoring him for a few hours. It worked.

But Wednesday after work, she had sat watching TV with Sam all evening. With nothing to do with her hands, she fidgeted for a while and then grabbed her computer and surfed the web for a while. Not finding anything that interested her, she shut the machine off and dragged Sam to the bedroom to take her mind off doing nothing. He was more than willing to keep her mind and body occupied for a time.

Thursday was much the same, so Sam suggested a run, and they did. After they got back, it was a shower together, then more TV. This time they watched a movie, but Natalie turned back to her computer since the movie was slow-moving and she was bored.

Friday, they had supper with her dad and Faith and the boys. Natalie liked her old art teacher, always had. Seeing her with her dad made Natalie wish that he had just told her years ago. They were very comfortable together, like they had been together for years. Of course, they had.

After supper, they all went into the back yard to play catch. With three growing boys, there was energy to burn. Even her dad and Faith had joined in the small game the tossing of the baseball had turned into. It was the most fun Natalie had in a few days.

But Saturday dawned with nothing for her to do. Nothing. Lying on the couch in the early afternoon, she wondered if Sam was ignoring her. When he had gone uptown to get groceries, she had mowed his lawn and her dad's. He seemed a little miffed it was done. Not happy she had done it for him like she had expected.

Now he was taking a shower, but she had already taken one after the lawn, so he was showering alone. Maybe he was miffed about that. He did enjoy sharing a shower. Maybe she needed another one?

Instead, she pulled out her phone and was paging through Facebook when he came out all clean and sexy. Looking at him from her spot on the couch, where her head was resting on the armrest, she whistled at him.

Turning to her, he asked, "Are you bored, Natalie?"

"Yes," she admitted in exasperation, dropping her phone on her chest.

Walking to her, he sat on a sliver of couch she was not on. She shifted a bit to give him more room. "What do you want to do?"

She raised an eyebrow at him.

He laughed at her. "What else do you want to do?"

"I don't know. I used to plan my wedding, but now I got nothing."

"You couldn't have planned your wedding every minute of every day." He ran a finger down her chest scar, pushing her shirt down as he did.

"No," she agreed. "I also worked at the library, and book club took some time. But mostly it was the wedding. You did not get to see my wedding, it was amazing."

"I got to see enough of it. I saw you." His finger had let her shirt go and touched her nose when he said 'you.'

"I had planned that baby to death. Maybe I should find someone getting married and plan their wedding. Tess? Ruth? But neither are even engaged." She sighed, *not even engaged.*

"Are you hinting at something?" he asked and picked up her hand that still wore the ring he gave her.

"No," she said quickly. It hadn't even dawned on her to get engaged. She was just liking being around him. "Are you thinking of that?"

"No, not yet. One day, but not yet. I do love that you wear my ring." He kissed it.

"I enjoy wearing it," she admitted with a grin.

Dropping her hand, he braced himself with his hand on the back of the couch and leaned down and kissed her. "You, Natalie Beckett, have a crazy amount of energy. What are we going to do about that energy?"

Running her hand up his chest, she said, "I have an idea."

"But then what would you do after that?" He laughed at her. "How about before the wedding planning? What did you do?"

"I was in school." She then ran her hand back down his chest.

"I am starting to think that you're not using your brain enough." He kissed her forehead.

"I want to do something, not think about something," she argued.

"When your mom said she skipped grades, I thought of you. You didn't try in school, you never needed to. So, you got in trouble and used your talents for evil, not good." He grinned at her.

"I did use up a lot of time thinking up ways to torture you," she admitted, sliding her other hand under his T-shirt.

"Your job doesn't stimulate your mind. You need something to make you think." He tapped her head with a finger.

"I know of something else that needs stimulation." She winked at him, and her hands trailed down his body.

"Later. Right now, I have an idea." He stood up and pulled her to her feet.

"But my idea is probably so much better." She wrapped her arms around him.

"Let me make a call, and I will meet you outside." He pushed her away and went to the bedroom.

Watching him go, she huffed out a breath. What was he thinking? Grabbing her tennis shoes on the way out of the house, she sat on the front step, putting them on. Slowly she tied them as she wondered if he was right. Was she not using her brain? Had she ever needed to? In high school, she hadn't really needed to study; once she had heard how to do it or listened to the lectures, she knew the information. It was just easy.

In college, she had dived in headfirst and overachieved because her body was still recovering. Maybe if she had applied herself like her mom had, she would have been something today. Not just a librarian, but a doctor or a lawyer. Smiling, she knew she had no interest in either of those things.

Looking down, she wondered what Sam was planning for her. Was she dressed OK? She was wearing black basketball shorts long enough to cover her scars and an orange Tigers T-shirt. It was Sam's, but she had not done laundry lately, and her clothes were getting limited. Maybe he was going to bring up the laundry thing.

Her hair was loose and long, and the breeze was making it go into her face as she waited, so she pulled the elastic band from around her wrist to put it up in a ponytail. He was taking forever.

When he came out, he was still in his shorts and t-shirt, so she was fine in what she had on. All he did was walk out the door and smile at her, keeping his secret to himself. Taking her hand, he started to walk away from the house.

After a few blocks, she couldn't stand it anymore. "Where are we going?"

"To the high school." He squeezed her hand.

"Why?"

"Do you want to play a little volleyball?" he asked from out of nowhere.

Squeezing his hand back, she said, "Oh, I think I can beat you at that."

His laugh made her smile—she loved that he was so easy to tease. That he didn't get mad at her for making fun of him. As they drew close to the school, she saw there were a few cars in the parking lot. Something must be going on today.

When they stepped onto the school property, the doors on the cars opened. Sam bumped her shoulder and said, "I'm not playing with you. These guys are."

Leaning into him, she asked, "And who are these guys?"

But he was busy pulling his keys out of his pocket as the girls approached them, calling out to him in welcome.

"Thanks for coming, ladies. This is my girlfriend, Natalie Beckett." He nodded at her, and her knees went a little weak. Girlfriend. They hadn't even talked about it, but she loved it. "Natalie is also Mr. Beckett's daughter. Natalie, this is Ava, Olivia, and Kylie. They're the captains of the volleyball team this year."

Shaking the girls' hands, she wondered what Sam was up to. Was he really thinking she could hold her own with three girls in their prime? She hadn't touched a volleyball in six years, and a lot had changed since then. All she could manage was, "Hi."

CHAPTER 21

SAM OPENED the door to the dark, quiet school, and the five of them went into the building. It was cooler than Natalie expected, but it smelled just like she remembered. Memories floated through her mind as he led them to the gym. Walking down the hallway past a bank of lockers, she almost reached out to touch one. Hanna's. It was right there, by Henry's and Hazel's. She was surprised they were still there. Her own one was nine lockers before; she was a B, they were Ms.

She knew she was falling behind the others, but she didn't care. This wasn't the first time she had been in the building since the Friday before the accident, but it was the first time she had been down this hallway when the building was nearly empty. Silent, like it was mourning too.

All those years ago, someone else cleaned out her locker. Someone else took down the pictures she had taped in there. Somebody else has used that locker—six other people now.

She forced herself to walk away from the memories. She couldn't go back to that day. She couldn't bring them back. They were just lockers now, someone else's lockers.

Stepping into the gym, she watched as Sam and the three girls set up the volleyball net. It was the same net she had put up dozens of times. She could help, but instead, she just looked around the brightly lit gym with all its memories.

Many hours of her youth had been spent in here. From being so little and playing during recess when it was too cold to go outside. It was this gym because the school was small enough to have been the school she'd attended from kindergarten to graduation, except she hadn't graduated here. The accident was too many months before graduation to get her diploma. Instead, she got her GED a year later.

It was also the gym she played every home game of volleyball and basketball, practiced nearly every day. All with Hanna and Hazel, who she had forced to stay in the sports that only Natalie herself was good at and loved. But they stayed because she'd asked.

Closing her eyes, she could see the bleachers full, and the announcer saying her name in a rolling cadence that echoed off the walls as she ran out onto the court every game. Opening them again, she saw the empty gym in front of her again, quiet.

Looking back at the girls who were done putting up the net, she turned to Sam. She had no idea if she could even play this anymore. Her body was different from the last time she had been here.

Sam walked up to her carrying a ball and handed it to her. As if he knew what she was thinking, he said, "Just try."

Smiling at him, she took the ball and walked further into the large room. Bouncing the ball like a basketball, she walked to the girls standing in a cluster by the net. "I haven't played in a while. I hope I don't embarrass myself."

They laughed with her, and one said, "I haven't touched a volleyball since November. I'll probably embarrass myself too."

"I wish I could say November. Try six years. So, take it easy on me."

They split into two groups, and as she took her position, she watched Sam leaving the gym. Letting her succeed or fail without him. Turning her back on him, she smiled at her partner Kylie. Bouncing the ball a few times then throwing it into the air, she served it, and it hit the net soundly. Then bounced to the ground. Kylie tossed it back to her, and she tried again. This time it went over the net like it was supposed to. As one of the other girls set the ball back, she forgot about her body's possible limitations and threw herself into the game.

By the end, she was exhausted, but it was a good feeling. She and Kylie had lost their game, but it didn't seem to bother the younger girl, so Natalie let it go as the four went to the stage at the end of the gym to sit down. The three younger women jumped up and sat on the edge, and Olivia asked, "Were you really going to play volleyball at NDSU?"

Surprised at the question, Natalie had almost forgotten the scholarship she had received a few days before the accident. Hence the drinking to celebrate. Nodding, she said, "Yes, and for basketball. I was going to try out for softball when I got there, but I never got there."

"I know." Kylie nodded. "Every year, we get the talk about drinking and driving. They always include pictures of your car."

Natalie's heart almost stopped. Her car. Her beautiful little red Ford Focus bought used and well-loved. The only thing she had added was a new stereo. Another victim of the accident. She was sure she never needed to see those pictures.

"It was worse than the car probably looks. So do not drink and drive, and always wear your seat belts. *Always*." Natalie looked at each of the girls, hoping beyond hope that they would never go through anything like she did.

"You look like you aren't any worse for wear," Ava stated. She was looking Natalie up and down.

"You remind me of me, Ava. Indestructible. But you're not. Neither am I," she said to all three. Then changed the subject. "Are you guys looking forward to senior year? You're all seniors, right?"

"Yup, this is the year," Olivia said with a smile.

"You guys were really good out there. Do you think you'll get very far?" Natalie asked. Landstad never went to state in sports; they were never that good. But sometimes, they came close.

"Nope, we have no coach, so we're not doing volleyball this year," Kylie answered from her spot on the stage.

"Coach Miller?" He had been the coach for as long as she could remember. Though she hadn't liked him much, she had respected him.

"Retired," Ava supplied. "And nobody else wants to coach us."

Realization dawned on her. Sam and his dirty tricks. He wanted her to coach, and they were short a volleyball coach, knowing that she would have a harder time saying no when she knew some of the girls. But she had no idea how to coach. Sure, she could play the game, but that was not the same thing as coaching it.

"Mr. Sullivan said you would maybe be able to coach us," Olivia stated.

"I've never coached before," she admitted to the three girls.

"Mr. Sullivan said you would figure it out. We've only two weeks before we have to start practicing for the season. Could you think about it?" Kylie asked.

Turning and looking around at the big gym behind her, she wondered if she could actually coach. She loved playing, but coaching would be completely different. Could she come up with plays and encourage the kids? Actually, she was worried that she would get too obsessed with it and push the kids too hard and be mad when they didn't perform.

"I'll think about it." She turned to the girls. "But you have to promise me something first." All three nodded at her. And she looked at these three girls, who had their entire future in front of them. However long or short it was. "When you get home, tell your parents you love them, then tell your friends. They'll all be gone one day, and you don't know when that day will be." She walked away from them, hoping that they didn't see her cry. But she had to say it. It was something her younger self should have heard, should have done.

They left quickly. She was sure she had scared them, but they needed to be scared. If things could change at any moment, they needed to know that this moment wouldn't last forever. One day it will all be behind them, and this will be a memory.

Walking around the gym, she looked at the giant Tiger head on the wall. It was there when she had played as well. *Looked as creepy then as it does now too,* she thought to herself. Faith should fix it. The entire gym looked the exact same as it had all her life. Nothing changes in Landstad. Well, it does, but not fast.

Wondering where Sam had gotten to, she wandered the halls she had not been in for years. They were the same. Peeking into her dad's science room, she couldn't see anything that had changed in the years she had been absent. Further down the hall was the history room. She saw Sam was at his desk reading. So cute sitting at his desk.

Opening the door, she leaned against it and said, "Well, isn't it sexy Sam at work. Doesn't he know it's summer?" She started to walk toward him. "Doesn't he know that nobody likes history? Well, except for the gorgeous teacher who teaches it."

Smiling at her, he leaned back in his chair as he watched her walk toward him. When she got to him, she sat on the corner of his desk right next to his chair. Looking over her shoulder, she saw that he was taking notes from the textbook open nearby.

"How was your game?" he asked and ran his hand up her leg.

"It was a dirty trick, Sullivan. That's what it was." She folded her arms in front of her.

"Just payback for the many you played on me, Beckett." He turned his chair so that it was more in front of her.

"I was thinking, Mr. Sullivan."

"Dangerous activity, Miss Beckett." He smiled up at her.

"Jerk! I was thinking that many years ago, you got to see Hanna and Hazel's boobs but never mine." Then she pouted at him.

"I wish I had seen yours instead." His hands slid under her shirt to cup them.

"I've been learning that you cannot change the past. But maybe seeing them today will be enough." She pulled her shirt over her head.

"Natalie," he said in warning and dropped his hands away from her.

"Oh shoot!" She looked down, ignoring his warning, and reached behind her. "I forgot about my bra."

"Natalie," he warned again, but he didn't sound as against it as she unclasped her bra and let it fall to the floor.

"Mr. Sullivan." Her eyes were looking into his, but his were not looking into hers.

"Natalie." His voice was a warning, but his smile said something else.

A door slammed somewhere in the building, and they both scrambled to grab her shirt. Once back on, their ears were straining to hear any other sounds. Neither heard anything as she worked to get her bra back on without taking her shirt completely off. It was a challenge.

Standing up, he kissed her as he closed the book on his desk. "Let's go before someone walks in on us."

Walking with him to the door, she asked, "Do you think that it would have ended with us leaving together if I had shown you my boobs at seventeen?"

Smiling, he said, "God, I hope not."

Sam took Natalie's hand in his as he left his classroom. They walked the hallway as he asked, "You didn't say if you were going to coach, Beckett."

"I don't know. I haven't really thought about it. I need to think about it." She watched him shut the lights off in the gym.

"You only have a few weeks to figure it out. But the sooner you do, the more time you have to think about what you're going to teach them." He took her hand again, and they walked back past the lockers.

Reaching out with her other hand, she skated her fingers over the cold metal of the three May kids' lockers, needing to feel something they had touched once again. Feel a physical connection where only an emotional one was. Dropping her hand back down to her side, she felt a little more at peace with them. At least two of them.

Out in the sunshine, she watched Sam lock the door of the school. It was warmer out now than when they had gone in, but the warmth felt good. Her body was getting sore from all the activity she had just done, so she would have to take a pain pill when she got home. But it was all worth it.

Sam took her hand as they started for his house. Their house? She felt it was her home with him. Stealing a look at him, she smiled. Her Mr. Sullivan. So far, she had hadn't found a good reason to move out, not that she was looking.

CHAPTER 22

The August afternoon sun was hot as Sam finished mowing his lawn. Natalie had just mowed it on Saturday, but it was supposed to rain for the next few days, and he didn't want it to get too long. He loved mowing his lawn; it relaxed him. When Natalie had done it for him earlier, he was a little upset, but then again, he had already been on edge with her nervous energy.

Looking over his little lawn, he was happy with the results: it was neat and trim and smelled of freshly cut grass. Now all he had to do was wait for Natalie to come home from the library, but that was still hours away.

Movement caught his eyes, and he waved at his neighbor, who was mowing his lawn today too. Patrick shut his mower off and waved Sam over. Leaving his mower where it was, he headed over to talk to his old friend.

He sat down at the patio table across from Natalie's father for the first time since the man's daughter had moved in with him. It should be more awkward than it was. Sam was glad Natalie had told him Patrick was more than okay with them being together. Falling for his friend's daughter behind the man's back was the last thing Sam wanted to do.

Wiping the sweat off his brow, he asked, "How is it going? Faith move in yet?"

"No, not yet. We're getting everything organized. We have two houses to fit into one. And a bunch of kids," Patrick said with a smile. Sam knew the kids were the least of Patrick's concerns.

"Just tell me when you need help to move stuff. I'll have Natalie come over and help you." He laughed when Patrick caught the joke.

"Good luck with that. She hasn't even moved anything of hers to your house." Patrick looked across the yard at his house.

Sam stopped laughing. She hadn't brought anything over, hadn't even asked. Did she feel she needed someplace to land if things didn't turn out? Most of her clothes were even still at her dad's house. She seemed more than okay to wear his clothes.

"How is Natalie? Jumpy?" Patrick asked.

Sam turned to the older man. "How did you know she would be jumpy?"

"Nervous energy. She's always been that way. In school, three sports were not enough sometimes. Was her mom that way?" Patrick asked with interest.

Sam wondered if he had asked anything more than what Natalie had told him about the woman, or if he had just let his daughter ramble when they had talked.

"No, not her mom. One of the sisters seemed a little like that, but maybe it came from the dad." Sam hated to say 'dad' because Patrick would always be her dad, even if someone else provided half her genes. "But her brains came from her mom."

"Natalie said she's a judge. I guess you have to be smart to be a judge."

"Yes, and she skipped grades and got through college in three years. I wonder if Natalie wasn't challenged enough in school. Maybe her mom was just able to focus the energy into something else." Sam stated his theory.

"I know she wasn't challenged, but I hated to push too much. Lara had her reading by three, but after she was gone, I didn't know what to do. If I had her skip grades, she would have lost her friends. By the last years of high school, she was physically busy but was still not mentally challenged. I don't even know if she has ever been mentally challenged," Patrick admitted and looked off into the back yard.

"I think her job bores her." Sam looked at the half-cut grass in Patrick's backyard, not at his friend.

"I know. I wanted her to do something else, but she said she could do this degree from a hospital bed, so she did. Once she sets her mind to something, there's no changing it," Patrick said on a sigh.

"I've asked her to coach the volleyball team," Sam told him, wondering if Natalie had talked to him about it already. They were close, after all.

"I know, she told me. She's thinking about it. I think she would be great at it, except she's very competitive. Too competitive sometimes."

Sam was shocked. So maybe the man did know of her faults. "Do you think she'll do it?" Sam knew the man knew her mind better than she did on some things.

"In the end, yes. She needs convincing and reassurance. I told her to talk to the one person who knows her best, see what they think."

"Hazel?" Questioned Sam.

"I didn't say who. We'll see who she talks to. But I have a feeling it will be her also," Patrick agreed.

"Will Hazel talk to Natalie?" Sam didn't know the answer to that.

"Maybe, maybe not. Hazel's not the same person I knew." Patrick had known the girl since she was five or six.

"Natalie said that she wasn't a great friend to Hazel. It's been bothering her lately." Sam remembered the pain in her green eyes when she had told him what Hazel had told her.

"I saw that back then. Hanna was always Natalie's best friend, but Hazel was always there. Hazel's best friend was also Hanna. It made it hard for Hazel. She wasn't as competitive as Natalie, and I'm afraid she let Natalie win and, in the end, lost more than her friend. Her sister. I just wish they could be friends again. I miss those days." Patrick pushed away from the table and stood up.

"They do too, Patrick." Sam got up as well, thinking about how much Hazel's reactions bothered Natalie.

Waving goodbye to his friend, he headed back to his house, grabbing his lawnmower on the way. After a quick shower without Natalie, he sat on the couch to wait for her to come home. Though her energy was draining sometimes, he loved having her live with him. They hadn't talked about it, but she never talked about going to stay at her dad's house. After the first night, she even parked in front of his place now, not going through the yards to her dad's house.

But it was worrying him that she wasn't moving her stuff over, just little things now and again. Maybe she wasn't as into living with him as he was. Once she figured out the coaching thing, he would have to talk to her about it.

CHAPTER 23

CLOSING the book as the story ended, Natalie leaned back in her chair. Looking at the cover again, she was so excited she couldn't contain it. But she had to because she was in the library.

Today the library had gotten the latest in the Z. Connor book series, and Natalie was the first to have read it—in less than two hours. She had been waiting for today since her mom had told her who the author was.

Flipping through the front of the book and then the back, she had never noticed there was no information on the author in this series. Most books were big on promoting their other works, but not this one. Smiling, Natalie looked around the library; nobody was looking at her, so she hugged the book to her chest.

Getting up to put the book back on the shelf, she wondered if Della could have her aunt send her a signed copy. Her aunt Zephyr, the author. Her aunt, who talked to her like she was just Della's little sister. Not a best-selling author with a movie about the first book in theaters.

Ruth was an author too, so it wasn't all that odd, but Natalie had been reading her aunt's books for years. She had every book in the series on the family room bookshelf. Soon she would have to dust them off so her new brothers could read the series she had so enjoyed.

She was glad she finished before she had to start the children's reading time; she hated to put a book down before she finished it. But today, she was reading one of her favorites, and she had asked Hazel to bring in John Henry. Natalie was a little nervous to see Henry's mirror image and her friend. Natalie hadn't seen Hazel since book club when she had said she was going to quit. So far, she hadn't talked to the rest of the group, feeling it was her who Hazel had an issue with. Not them. But today, she wanted to talk to the person who knew her best. Besides her dad, that was Hazel, and she would tell Natalie how it was. Hazel doesn't hold back in case it hurt her feelings.

As Natalie grabbed the book she was reading to the kids off her desk, she caught Hazel coming in out of the corner of her eye and sighed with relief that she had actually come. Now she would have to get her to talk to her.

Taking her seat in front of the children, she noticed that John Henry had sat in the back. He wasn't outgoing and active like some little boys. His personality reflected his mom's: quiet and reserved.

Natalie had memorized the children's book years ago, so she looked around the library to see if Hazel was there as she read the story out loud. Of course, she didn't leave. She would never leave John Henry alone. Her friend was in the library somewhere.

Closing the book, she got up to make sure Hazel didn't sneak out before she could talk to her. Watching where John Henry ran, Natalie followed, and she found Hazel in the kid's section, reading a book that was not from the children's section. John Henry climbed onto her lap, and she quickly closed the book on Jeffrey Dahmer.

"Hazel, can I talk to you?" Natalie asked as Hazel started to get up.

"I thought that you were just being nice inviting John Henry to listen to a book. But you actually were just using him. So, no," Hazel accused.

"Please, Hazel, I just want to talk. Nothing about the accident."

Hazel looked at her for a while before replying, "Fine, five minutes."

"John Henry will be fine out here alone for a few minutes," Natalie said since the boy had gone to see what another boy was looking at on the bookshelf. Leading her to a meeting room, she closed the door behind them.

Neither spoke for a while. It wasn't easy to start. There was always too much between them. Too much that needed to be said. Too much that couldn't be said.

"Do you want to sit?" Natalie asked.

"No." Hazel leaned against the door, glancing out the window that looked out at the rest of the library to see John Henry still playing.

"I will." Natalie sat on the edge of the table, feeling uncomfortable sitting while Hazel stood, angry. "I want to talk about high school."

"I thought you said we wouldn't talk about the accident?" Hazel's hand went around the doorknob.

"Not about the accident. About me in high school," Natalie assured her.

"What do you want to know?" Hazel's eyes were on the floor between them as her hand stayed on the knob.

"Was I a bad person? You know, all around? Mean to people and hard to get along with?" Natalie knew Hazel would know. She was there.

"Sometimes. I think we all were then. You were …" She paused. "You were you, outgoing and opinionated about everything. I think you thought you were better than everyone. I mean, you were. You were smart and funny and good at sports. But you were also a little self-centered and treated the rest of us like we were in the way."

Natalie had expected her to be truthful, but she didn't think the truth would hurt so much. Had she really been that cocky kid Hazel was describing? But she knew she was. Hazel might not like her much, but she wouldn't lie to her. That was not who Hazel was.

"Is that why you stopped hanging out with us the last year?" Natalie asked, hoping it wasn't her that pushed Hazel away before the accident even happened. Because looking back, she could see Hazel had stopped being there. At some point, she had stopped being around.

"No, Hanna didn't want me there anymore. She said I was a drag and wasn't any fun. That she had gotten tired of being told to include me. That I should find my own friends. You were her friend." Hazel let the tears fall from her eyes, not even wiping them away all the time.

"When did she say that?" Natalie did wipe hers away. Never realizing her best friend could be so cruel to her own sister. That she hadn't seen it.

"That summer. Before the fourth sometime. I don't remember exactly. I didn't hang out with you guys after that. I stayed home just like she wanted," Hazel said, looking at her shoes.

"But you hung out at school? I remember you being with us," Natalie said, though maybe she hadn't been there as much in school either.

"Because I had no other friends. You were my friends. You two just didn't want me around anymore." Looking up, her hazel eyes were full of pain and brimming with tears.

"I was your friend. The whole time." Natalie wanted to hug her friend but knew she couldn't. Hazel would be gone if she moved.

"You always tried to include me, but when Hanna said I was busy or didn't want to go, you let it go. So, I stayed home and let you be friends without me," Hazel whispered the last bit.

"Is that why you didn't do volleyball that fall?" Natalie asked. It was the only year Hazel hadn't played alongside her. At the time, she hadn't thought much about it. Now she did.

"Yes and no. Hanna asked me not to play since I wasn't any good. But you always yelled at me, so I didn't have fun anyway. It was supposed to be fun." Hazel shrugged.

"Was I that bad? I don't remember yelling at you." Natalie racked her mind for any time.

"Yes, all the time. Once the game started, you were always yelling at someone. Sometimes at practice even. You always forgot it was supposed to be fun. It wasn't fun to play with you."

Natalie was starting to hate her younger self. Maybe the accident changed her more than she thought. She would have to look at the game tapes her dad made over the years and see how bad she was. "I've been asked to coach the volleyball team this fall, but I have to turn it down. If I was that bad back then, how can I coach anyone now?"

Hazel looked up at her in confusion. "Because you've changed, Natalie. You're not that person anymore. You know that it's just a game now. Life is short, and the game has no bearing on it."

"You don't know me now. What if I haven't changed?" Natalie asked, not sure if what Hazel said was true. Had she changed?

"Because I spend four hours every two weeks with you. The old you would never have been in book club. You would never have given Mia, a waitress, and Ruth, a secretary, a chance to be your friend. And you rarely take over the conversation and not let anyone talk or tell everyone your opinion without letting others argue with you. You're not the old Natalie." Hazel glanced out the door at her son again.

"So, you think I could do it?" she asked again.

"As long as you remember that it's a game, winning and losing isn't important. Having fun is. Play the kid who doesn't always make the basket or hit the ball. They want to have fun too. Watching every game from the bench doesn't make you feel like you're part of the team," Hazel replied, who sat on the end of the bench at every game they ever played together. "And don't yell at them. They know they messed up; they don't need you telling them that they did."

"You should be the coach, Haze," Natalie said with a smile at her insight. The tears were still there, though.

"I hate sports. I only did it to be with my friends." She rolled her eyes and then checked her son, who had moved on from the other boy and was sitting alone, looking at his mom across the room. "I have to go."

Watching her leave, Natalie was happy she had gotten to actually talk to Hazel. Her dad had been right, she needed to talk to the person who knew her best.

Before the talk, she had thought the hardest thing would be

teaching plays and strategy to teenagers. She knew she could yell, but she thought it would be an asset as a coach. Now she realized who she had been all those years ago. Who she didn't want to be today. But what she didn't know was how to not be that person again.

CHAPTER 24

BY THE END of the day, Natalie still hadn't figured out if she wanted to coach or not. Or actually, she had. She wanted to coach the team, but she still didn't know if she should. She didn't want to be the coach who yelled at everyone, and nobody liked. Looking back on her coaches, she knew she wanted to be the coach that kids liked and looked up to. The kind that you could talk to and wanted to talk to.

So, before she went to Sam's, she went to her dad's house. At the patio door, she wondered if she should knock. This had been her home, but it wasn't anymore. Even the years she had been in Fargo, this had still been her home. But now, that was across the back yard from where she felt at home.

With a deep breath, she slid open the patio doors and walked into the kitchen. Her dad was making supper and looked up at her. "I didn't think I would see you today. How was your day?"

"Good … OK … I don't know." She stumbled over her usual answer. Hazel's words still ran through her head. Stopping one step into the house, she asked, "Should I knock?"

"If you want to. You're always welcome." Her dad set down the spoon he was holding.

"I know, it just feels like I should knock. It's weird," she admitted.

"You do whatever you want," the always agreeable Patrick said.

"I think I will next time. See what that feels like. Maybe I'll knock and then just come in."

"Did you just come here to talk about knocking?" her dad asked with a smirk.

"No, I need a few things. Again. And I want to borrow some of my volleyball tapes. More than just senior year," she added so she could see Hazel again, see if she really yelled at her friend all the time.

"Going to review your career before coaching?" her dad asked and followed her through the house to the bedroom area.

"No, not really. I talked to Hazel today, and she said I yelled at her a lot." She grabbed the things she needed from her bedroom. Her dad was in his office next door.

Her dad appeared in the door holding a box of little disks. "I can tell you right now you did. Did you want to see it?"

Tentatively, she took the box from his arms, his words worrying her. Did he think she was a bad person too? She was afraid she was going to see how bad she was. "I need to know. I don't remember it that way."

Turning, her dad led her to his office. Grabbing a few more discs off the shelf behind him, she wondered how many hours of her life had actually been recorded. But she knew it was a lot. He added the disked to the box and said, "You'll want to watch these too."

"Am I?" she wondered out loud.

"Maybe. Your choice." Her dad gave her a quick hug.

"Thanks, Dad. Thanks for recording my life so I can just review it at any moment. The good and bad." Giving him a one-armed hug back, she knew she was about to see the bad. And sadly, at the time, it had felt like it was so good.

"I wouldn't change it for the world, even if you hated me for doing it," he admitted as they went back to the kitchen. "Do you want to stay for supper?"

"No, Sam's probably making something for us already. Is it weird yet, Sam and I?"

"Sam and me, sweetheart." Her dad smiled at his grammar joke.

"No, not weird. I like him, and I like him for you. What do you think of Faith and me?"

"I'm just happy for you. You deserve to be happy." She smiled at him.

"That's how I feel about you and Sam. I can see he makes you happy." Her dad pulled open the sliding door for her.

"Happier than I thought possible not that long ago." She kissed his cheek as she left the house.

"That's what I've always wanted for you. Someone who makes you happy." He closed the door.

Back across the yards, she slipped through Sam's back door. As she closed it, she wondered if she would have to shovel a path through the snow to her dad's house in the winter. But she knew she gladly would. Kicking off her shoes, she dropped the box on the coffee table and went to change clothes, bringing the few personal items she took from her room with her.

Putting the items away, she slipped out of her work clothes and hung them up, then dressed in some leggings and a T-shirt before going back to the living room. Sam was still missing, so she wondered if she could head back to her dad's later for a meal. That would be far easier than her making something.

Setting her phone on the coffee table, she saw he had sent her a text she had missed that he was at the grocery store. Since she had a few minutes, she put a movie in the DVD player. Volleyball against Campbell, their biggest rival when she was a junior. There she was. The camera was focused on her most of the time, but it would sometimes catch Hazel or Hanna as they were playing. Except for the numbers on their backs, they were indistinguishable. They looked so much alike. It was before Hazel had cut her hair off, and they were styled the same.

But almost from minute one, she heard herself yelling at her teammates. Pointing out their errors and showing her disappointment in them. Never did she congratulate, always just negative. As if she hadn't made a single mistake in her life.

Tired of watching herself yelling at the people she missed so much, she removed the disk and replaced it with another. Not sports this time, since she knew now how bad of a person she was. This time it was a dance video—whatever that was.

The moment she saw the three of them on the screen, she knew what dance. It was junior prom, her only prom. Her date had been Henry while Hanna went with a boy from a neighboring town, and Hazel hadn't gone at all. But she did spend the day helping the other two get ready. Just trying to be involved as best she could.

Natalie remembered the pink dress she had to have. Nothing else would do. Hanna was in red, but she barely remembered that. Hazel was in jeans and an oversized sweatshirt that was Henry's since it was cold in North Dakota in early April.

Her dad had recorded some of their getting ready. Natalie and Hanna were chatting about what fun the dance was going to be and who was going to be there. Including a few barbs at Hazel for not going, not being able to find a date. Then they spent some time just talking about what Hazel had to do to get a date: loosen up, grow up, be more outgoing, be more like them.

Sitting alone on the couch, she wanted to yell at her younger self that it was easy for her to say, she had just started dating her best friends' brother, no big risk. Hanna was no better. She had only gone out with that guy three times for that dance and never again afterward. From the couch, she could see how the words had hurt Hazel. Now, seven years later, Natalie could see how her words hurt those she loved.

From the couch, she watched herself finish getting ready for the dance, getting in her car, the one from the accident, with Henry, Hanna, and a guy she couldn't even remember the name of. The group was all smiles, but instead of focusing on them, she watched Hazel getting into her car in the background, going home alone.

Jumping up, she took out the disk. She couldn't watch anymore. Dropping it in the box, she saw the next one was labeled Graduation. Picking it up, she slid it into the player and watched Hazel May graduate from high school. Sure, she knew everyone who graduated that day, but she only saw Hazel.

On the screen was not the shy, quiet girl from school, but nor was it the Hazel she had talked to today. In front of her was a shell of those versions. Her hair was cut short, not as short as now, but no longer just barely touching her shoulders like she had been wearing for years. Shorter than Natalie had seen ever seen it. The cut was terrible, and Natalie was sure that no stylist had been involved. Her once-bright eyes were sunken, her skin looked gray, and the orange gown did nothing to make her look any better.

Hazel had said she missed a lot of school that year and that Sam had helped her get her diploma signed. She could see why. The person on the screen was barely alive.

Even from a distance and years later, Natalie could see that she didn't want to be there. That, like church every Sunday, someone was forcing her. And being Hazel, she did what was expected of her.

To honor the students that lost their lives that day, they had left empty chairs that they would have sat in. They were covered in garments, but the chairs were empty. Since Hazel's name came between Hanna and Henry's names alphabetically, she sat alone between the two empty chairs. Another reminder that she was now alone, that they were gone.

By the time Sam walked through the door, she was a puddle on the couch, unable to even turn off the movie. She had still been trapped in a hospital bed when it had happened, not even thinking about the day she had dreamed of for long. And if she had, all she could think about was how her friends were moving on with their lives. Thinking she was the only one who wasn't. Except now she knew that Hazel wasn't either. Hazel still hadn't.

But it didn't matter what was on the screen, she couldn't see it. Between the tears in her eyes and the new memories she had seen today, she was not seeing anything. Not even Sam when he sat down and gathered her into his arms. His big, strong arms couldn't protect her from who she had been. A monster.

CHAPTER 25

HIS HEART STOPPED when he walked in from the garage with an armful of groceries and found her sitting on the couch racked with sobs. Her entire body was shaking, and her breathing was ragged as her eyes were locked on the TV screen. He didn't even think she knew he came into the house. Glancing at the screen, he saw a high school graduation playing on the screen, and it took only a second for him to figure out which one.

"Natalie, what are you doing? Are you okay?" He pulled her into his arms as he sat down.

"No, I'm not," she whispered through her tears, trying to get closer to him than she was.

"Are you watching your graduation?" he questioned as he ran a hand over her black hair, but he didn't need to ask. He knew.

"Hazel," was all she said and sobbed again.

"You shouldn't watch this." Turning the TV off, he wished he had come home sooner before she had turned it on. He had been at that graduation and had barely made it through. For weeks he had tried to talk the principal out of leaving the chairs empty, to think about the remaining triplet. But there was no getting through to him, and he had watched Hazel the entire time. As had so many.

"I have to. I needed to know," she whispered into his shirt.

"Need to know what?" he questioned, his arms tightening around her.

"How bad of a person I was," she whispered again through her tears.

"You were not a bad person."

"I saw me. I was. Hazel said so. Hazel knows me." The sobs started again.

"Natalie, you were a kid then. You have grown up. You're not that person anymore." He rubbed her back and kissed her head in comfort.

"But what if I still am?" she asked, the sobs slowing.

"You're not," he argued.

"How do you know?" she questioned with only tears running down her face.

"Because I could never love a bad person, but I love you." He hadn't planned on telling her that until a better time, a better place. But it was out now.

"You can't love me. You don't know how mean I am."

"I knew you before the accident and after. I know you pretty well." He wiped the tears from her cheeks.

"But Hazel said, and she knows me," she stated.

"Did Hazel say you were a bad person now? Or just back then?"

"Back then. She said I've changed," she whispered.

"You have. So much so that you don't even recognize who you were before. Not only did the outside change after the accident, so did the inside." He lightly kissed her wet, salty lips then pulled her back tight to him.

Looking up from her, he saw a box of little disks on the coffee table. How long had she been sitting here reliving her life, seeing all her flaws? He cursed his friend for recording so much of her life. Some things don't need to be relived years later. Most things from your teenage years deserve to just be lost to time.

Reaching down on the ground, he dug through the bag at his feet and pulled out something he had bought for her. "Ice cream?"

"You know that is a cliché. But I need a spoon." Grabbing the container, she opened it as he went to the kitchen and grabbed one.

He handed it to her before he sat down and pulled her back into his arms. Quietly, she ate the cold treat, her eyes still on the black screen of the TV.

"Does the ice cream make you feel better?" He pulled her attention from the past again.

"Yes. It shouldn't, though." He let her feed him a spoonful of ice cream.

"So why the movie marathon today?" Taking the spoon from her, he ate a bite of cold minty ice cream.

"Hazel said I had yelled at her a lot when we played sports. I didn't remember that." She looked at the black TV screen.

"And now?" He knew she had already watched it. Hazel was right; he had been to enough of her games to have seen it firsthand.

"I was awful. If I coach, I don't want to be like that." She ate another bite.

"You won't do that. When you were playing with Della's girls, they messed up all the time, and you said nothing. Just helped them. Then when we were playing kickball with the entire family, the rules weren't even followed, but you just let it happen and had fun. And did you yell at anyone the other day playing volleyball?"

"No," she answered, but he could feel her mind was elsewhere.

"Did Hazel tell you not to coach?" He knew she would have asked.

"No, she said I would be good at it. Just to not take it too seriously. Just have fun," Natalie admitted, her concentration on her ice cream.

"I think Hazel is right. You need to look at this as a fun thing, to not take it too seriously. If you win, you win, but if you lose, you still had fun." He kissed her hair.

"Thank you, Sam. For everything you have done for me." She leaned more into him.

"I'm glad I took you home after the wedding. My life has made a change for the better since that day." He kissed her head again.

"Even if I cry a lot? And I mean a lot." Natalie put the ice cream on the coffee table.

"Are you going to cry again?" he asked, watching her turn to look at him.

"No. I just want to look at you." She touched his cheek gently.

"Why?" he asked, looking into her green eyes.

"Because I think you said you loved me when I was sobbing on the couch. Not the time to tell a girl that."

"I think I did too."

"Will you say it when I'm not crying?" she asked, still looking him in the eyes.

"No, I will not. Only when you're crying." His words were barely out before she attacked him, pushing him over.

Laughing, he grabbed her into his arms before she could push him off the couch.

"You are a jerk, Mr. Sullivan."

Holding her tight as she tried to wiggle free, he replied, "And I love you, too, Natalie Beckett."

Pulling her to him so he could kiss her, she kissed him back. Repositioning herself, she was straddling him, then she pulled away a little. Looking into his eyes, she touched his forehead with hers and said, "I love you, sexy Sam."

Running his hands up her back, he fought the urge to slide the shirt up her body. "When are you moving in then?"

She pulled back more and looked at him closely. Her green eyes pierced his in confusion. "I am moved in."

"You have almost nothing here."

She looked around at the room. "I don't have much."

"So, if I went to your dad's, there would be nothing in your bedroom?" he asked.

"I have some clothes, but I was waiting for Faith's kids to move in, then I'll take it all."

"Why not now?" he questioned.

"Right now?" She bit her lip.

"Right now," he challenged.

"Why can't I just move it over here when I find space for it?" She looked around the room again.

"How much do you have?" he questioned. He had no idea. Maybe it was a lot.

"Almost nothing. And most of is just … kid stuff." Her nose wrinkled at the words.

"Kid stuff?"

"Yeah, like a lamp that has unicorns on it, a picture of cats … I didn't buy anything because Jason had everything already. The apartment I lived in before moving back was furnished. I don't really have anything."

"You have all your clothes here?" He was sure she didn't. He had cleaned out a good-sized area in his closet, and she didn't have much in it.

"Mostly. Well, I don't have the winter stuff here. It's summer, you know. I have what I wear. I don't have a lot of clothes. I'm not a big shopper, never have been."

"Why do you constantly steal my shirts?" He touched the blue shirt she was wearing.

"Because I hate doing laundry, and these smell like you." She lifted the hem and smelled the shirt she was wearing, giving him a glimpse of her stomach scars as she did it. Even today, seeing her scars turned him on, because he knew she didn't show them to just anyone.

"It just seems like you have nothing here. Like it's only temporary," he told her.

"I'm not going anywhere. I just put the stuff I bring here away as I bring it. Do you want me to bring the unicorn lamp so that you know I'm staying?" She ran her fingers through his hair.

"Maybe, if it's all you have." He pulled her closer to him.

"I have books, but they're on my dad's bookshelf in the basement. I want to leave them. The shelves would be empty without them. Dad doesn't read." She slid her hands down his back.

"Are you sure you're staying?" he questioned again, needing to hear her say it again.

"Forever and ever. Just try and get rid of me." She wiggled on his lap.

Flipping her down so that her back was on the couch, he said, "I am never going to get rid of you. I saved you twice just so I can have you forever."

CHAPTER 26

WATCHING the last student leave his classroom, Sam was glad the first day of school was over. Though he loved teaching, the first day after summer break was hard. The kids were great, but no one was ready to sit all day, and everyone was antsy, as antsy as the woman he loved.

Though over the last few weeks, her energy had been focused on coaching volleyball, which had helped. This week he started to push her to think about taking some online courses. She wasn't completely on board yet, but she was considering it.

"Did you bore anyone to death today with history?" Natalie said from the door. He hadn't even noticed she was there. Today she was dressed in an orange polo shirt with a little tiger on it. The black dress pants looked different on her—he hadn't seen her in anything other than shorts and skirts since they got together. He missed her long legs on display. At least he would get to see them every night.

"I am a very exciting teacher teaching an exciting subject." He sat on the top of one of the desks. If he got too close to her, he would have to touch her, kiss her. Today the building was full of kids—impressionable kids.

"Keep telling yourself that, Sullivan. Do you like the shoes? They came today." She pointed at the orange tennis shoes on her feet that were a perfect match to her shirt. So out there and so Natalie.

"I love them. Are you nervous?" Today was not only his first day of school for the year but her very first game of coaching. In a few hours, she would be leading the volleyball team to victory or defeat.

"Nervous, no. I'm scared to death. Why did I even sign up for this? What do I know about sports?" she rambled and walked into his room.

"You know everything about it. You'll be great. Once it gets going, you'll forget everything else." Getting up, he took her hand in his and smiled at her scared green eyes.

"Maybe," she mumbled.

"Did you tell Della about your big game?" he asked to distract her.

"Yes. She said good luck. I got texts from her sisters, too," she said with a smile.

As he had thought since meeting them, the Harts had embraced Natalie as one of their own, including her in everything. That included calls from her mom nearly daily now. And her aunts had included her in a group text that kept her updated on everything in their lives.

"I got you a present." He got up and went to his desk in the front of the room.

"A present? I didn't think we were doing presents. I mean, you never got me anything for my birthday." She followed him in her orange shoes.

"I got you a mom, isn't that enough?" he countered as he grabbed the gift bag from his desk drawer.

"No, I need more. Maybe another trip to your parents. Without them, if possible." She laughed because his parents were hinting that they needed to go back again. That they could have a big gathering there for some special event. Though no specific event had been mentioned. The hints made it sound like an engagement party.

"I don't think this will be as good as the one you got yesterday. So don't think it will be that great." He held the bag close to his chest.

There had been a box from Aunt Zephyr waiting for her when she got home from work. When she had opened it, she squealed and danced around the room. Her aunt was an author and had sent her copies of all her books, signed just for Natalie. Natalie loved her books before she knew the author was related to her. And now she had signed copies. It was an apology of sorts for saying the wrong thing the night they had left Birch Cove. Not that it was Zephyr's fault. Natalie was going to bolt no matter what. Sam knew that now.

He laughed at her enthusiasm as she grabbed the bag from him. Watching her open the bag and pull out a small box, her eyes met his over the bag. "Are you proposing?" her breathless voice asked.

"Am I?" He pulled her into his arms and kissed her. He was not, but he loved her reaction.

Pushing him away, she opened the box. Her face showed she was a little let down. It was not a ring. Taking the box from her, he took the necklace it held and made her turn around.

"Lift up your hair," he whispered into her ear from behind.

As she did, he carefully put the necklace on, kissing her neck when the tiny clasp connected on her warm skin. Her head had tipped, exposing her neck, so he kissed it. Sliding his arms around her, he pulled her close to him with one arm, and the other hand touched the necklace he had just placed there. Whispering in her ear, he said, "It's a four-leaf clover for luck on your big game, and it has orange stones all around it because you are and always will be a Tiger."

He felt her melt into his body with a sigh. "God, I love you."

"I love you too, Natalie. Even when you're making fun of me." He chuckled at her when she slapped his leg.

He pulled away from her and turned her in his arms. "So, you want me to ask you to marry me?"

"It was just a thought. No rush." She was blushing, something she rarely did.

Soon after the night she watched herself on film from her high school days, she had moved her lamp over. She was right, it was a unicorn. But it meant she was staying. And he was planning to ask her soon, but not here, not now. He was going to marry this woman.

"How about this weekend we go shopping for some things for the house, and we can glance in a few jewelry stores. No rush. Just see what you like." He watched her eyes light up at the idea.

"That sounds fun," she said more to herself then to him.

"You are fun. I can't believe you're mine." He kissed her again, loving that she was his.

CHAPTER 27

SLOWLY, the gym filled up with fans for the first volleyball game of the year. Natalie scanned the bleachers, finding the book club sitting as a group on the top row. Seeing that she was looking at them, they all waved, and Mia let out a wolf whistle, making Natalie laugh. That caused her to relax for a moment.

Watching her players warm up from near their bench, she noticed her dad come into the gym in his old Landstad Tigers sweatshirt. She knew her name was written on the back of it because it had once been hers. With him was Faith and the boys, all decked out in the school colors of orange and white. Catching his eyes, she gave him a small wave, and he gave her a smile back. He wouldn't miss her first game of coaching.

Her first game, and she was nervous. She had no idea what the team was like last year, and she had no idea if her coaching was any good. From where she stood, the girls all looked happy and excited to show off their skills.

"Are you nervous?" She had been so lost in thought she hadn't noticed her dad come up beside her.

"Yes. But once the game gets going, I think I'll be okay," she admitted.

"You'll be great. You always are." He squeezed her shoulder in support.

"You never notice my failures." Smiling at him, she wrapped her arms around him for an actual hug.

"You never fail in my eyes, Natalie." He hugged her back.

Looking down at her dad, she told herself not to cry. Coaches didn't cry.

"Where's the camera?" she asked. He wasn't carrying the camcorder that was always with him.

"I did that because she wasn't in your life. Now she is, and it's up to her to come to your big events. I can't keep recording them for her." It seemed his job was suddenly over.

"It's a long way, and this isn't a big event, Dad."

"Every event is a big event to me." Turning, he looked at the seats behind her.

Following his lead, she turned to see what he was looking at— Faith and the boys sitting with Sam in the stands right behind her. "Go sit down with your girlfriend, old man. Keep your hands to yourself, too. Don't embarrass me." She bumped his hip with hers and laughed. It was still a little weird that he had a girlfriend and that she lived with him. Maybe that was why he didn't say anything about her living with Sam.

"Good luck." He walked away.

Looking at the clock, she called the girls into a huddle. When all the girls were there, she heard Mia let out another wolf whistle and yell out her name. Looking up in the stands, she looked right at Mia and touched her finger to the side of her nose, the sign during recording to be quiet. She saw Mia laugh at the sign and then sit down.

"I think you have more fans here than we do, Coach Beckett," Olivia said, and Natalie laughed.

Since that day in the gym, she had gotten to know the girls pretty well. In fact, she liked them a lot. They were a great group, and she was happy she got to be their coach. "Maybe this time, but next time they'll be here for you," she admitted.

"Yeah, right," Kylie said with a smile.

"Remember, have fun first, win second. No telling someone that they made a mistake. They already know and don't need to hear it from you. Right?" All the girls nodded. Natalie looked at Hazel sitting in the stands. The rule was for her, but since they hadn't talked alone since the library, Hazel didn't know about it yet.

The girls all agreed and yelled 'Tigers!' as the huddle broke and went back to stretching. Turning to grab her clipboard, she caught something out of the corner of her eye and looked quickly back to the entry door. Her mouth went agape when Della, Max, and the girls walked into the gym, all wearing Tiger wear. Della saw her and waved as Faith's youngest led them to where her dad and Sam were sitting.

As Max and the girls went and sat down, Della came over to where Natalie was standing. Her mother was in black tailored pants, four-inch heels and a white sweatshirt with a tiger head on it, and she was rocking it.

They hugged, and Mia let out another wolf whistle, and this time, Tess yelled her name. Again, she looked at them only to touch her nose, and they quieted down.

Turning back to her mom, she said, "You didn't have to come."

"Of course, I did. I never got to see you play, but I will get to see you coach," Della said.

"But it's a long way for a few minutes," Natalie argued.

"Natalie, I would drive across the country to watch you do nothing. I missed twenty-four years of your life, and I don't plan to miss anymore." Della hugged her again.

The announcer started to say the game was starting, so Della left her side and went to sit down.

Natalie noticed she went right to her dad, and they hugged before she sat and then just started to talk, but both were looking at her.

Her players hurried over, and her starting group stood beside her as the announcer, who was the same announcer who had announced all her games when she was in high school, announced the girls. Lance Kelley had always loved to tease her. When all the starting girls were announced for both teams, he announced the coach from the opposing team, and as she walked over to shake the woman's hand, she heard, "The coach for the Landstad Tigers is our very own Natalie Beckett, who is coaching her first game tonight."

Heart pumping like she was sixteen again, her name rolled through the gym and reminded her of all the nights her name had been said years ago. Natalie couldn't hear what the woman said to her as the crowd started to yell. She knew Mia was behind the yelling frenzy. Biting her lip, she turned around so she could see Sam, who was standing and clapping with her family beside him.

Had he realized how this would affect her?

Quickly the game got underway, and she forgot everyone was there and focused on the game—just like she had in high school, calling plays and paying attention to what the other team was doing. She noticed nothing around her, just the action in front of her. Did Mia whistle again? She didn't even know.

Their team lost at the end of the game, but not by much, and it was a promising sign for the year to come. Though she was sad they had lost, she was relieved that her first coaching game was over. Her girls were perfect, even if they didn't win. The win would have been great, but having fun was more important. Glancing up at Hazel, she saw her friend give her a thumbs up. It was a sign she didn't know she needed until she saw it. Hazel thought she had done well. Somehow, that was better than any win tonight would have been.

Hazel was still haunted by the accident, but Natalie was finally breaking away from the emotions of it. It would always be a part of her life, and those who were lost would always be in her mind. But like today, Natalie was able to get through a day without them constantly on her mind.

Natalie watched the girls walk off the court but not toward her. They just went to the end of the court, and the girls on the bench left to stand with them. Giving them a quizzical look, they all looked away from her gaze.

Turning to Lance, who had asked for everyone's attention, she saw he was looking right at her. "We at Landstad High would like to take a moment to thank Coach Beckett for coaching this team. Most of you know that after Coach Miller left, volleyball was going to be dropped due to a lack of coaching staff for the team. But we were lucky enough to get our own Natalie Beckett"—he made her name roll through the building again—"back to coach these fine girls. Maybe not to victory today, but soon. Can I get a cheer for Coach Beckett?"

The crowd around her erupted, and she waved at her dad, Della, and their families behind her. Turning, she waved at the book club across the gym, who were standing and cheering. Mia let out a wolf whistle, and Tess joined her with one of her own. Laughing, Natalie should have known Tess could make that noise also. Tess was full of secrets she only revealed when she wanted to.

"Natalie, can I have you out on the floor for a moment?" She turned back to Lance Kelley in confusion, but he used his hands to motion her to the middle of the floor. Were they going to present her an award or give her flowers? She had only coached one game, and maybe they were making too big of a deal about it. As she walked, she heard him continue. "Now Natalie was on her way to playing basketball and softball for the University of North Dakota when her life changed. But now we have you back in Landstad and hope that you will continue coaching for our girls in many sports."

Natalie was starting to feel all the eyes on her. Was there an actual point to this, or was Lance Kelley getting her back for something? Sweeping her eyes over the crowd, they were just sitting and listening to him talk. When they turned their heads, she followed, and saw Sam get up and walk out to her. Maybe he was coming to save her.

"Tonight is a first for me, but when Mr. Sullivan asked for a favor, of course I said yes," Lance was saying as Sam made it to her and pulled her into his arms for a hug.

"I love you," he whispered in her ear. Then he let her go, and to her shock, went down on one knee. Was he wanting to huddle in the middle of the gym floor, just the two of them in front of everyone? Her breath stopped when she saw he was holding a ring. She slammed a hand over her mouth at the scene before her, finally realizing what was happening. All her family being there for a game that was nothing to them. The book club coming, not that they wouldn't have supported her anyway.

Lance's voice broke through her thoughts. "Are you going to say yes, Coach Beckett?"

She turned to Sam and said as loud as she could, "Yes!"

Sam got up and lifted her into his arms, and spun her around the center of the court. The crowd cheered, and Natalie heard Mia's whistle again.

This time she didn't look for them in the crowd as Sam's mouth crushed hers, and she heard, "People, mark your calendar for April 24th. It was her parents' anniversary. And plan to attend, she has a tendency to run."

Pulling away from his kiss, she said, "I could never run from you, sexy Sam. Never."

And his mouth covered hers again.

CHAPTER 28

HERE SHE WAS AGAIN, standing in the basement of a church in a white dress. But this time, there was no panic, no worries. Mia was rushing back from upstairs, doing her check, pushing Natalie into the back room as she came with her information. Again.

"Your mom is here, or I think she is. There's a redhead sitting next to your dad. I'm going with that's her. But there are quite a few redheads, so still iffy on if that is her," Mia said as she jumped up onto the table to sit and wait. Just like before, but more relaxed.

"Good. Mom and Dad are here, and that's all I need to know." She leaned against the table with Mia. Today she could barely remember the panic of the summer before. She was marrying Sam Sullivan come hell or high water, and since it wasn't raining, high water wasn't likely. Even if the snow was melting and filling in the low spots with water, she was in no way worrying this time.

There were still another fifteen minutes before the wedding started. Only fifteen long minutes to get this thing over with so she could finally be married to Sam. She remembered her last wedding, where the wedding was the big event, and the marriage was the scary part. This time neither were bothering her, except she wanted to get the wedding over with so they could just be married—and off on a honeymoon.

"Did you want to go out the window? You fit." Mia pulled a bottle of whiskey out from a bookshelf she could reach from her spot on the table.

Laughing at her friend, she hugged her. "No, it hasn't even crossed my mind."

Mia handed her the bottle, and she took a drink, then handed it back. "So, he's the one?"

"Oh, yes," was all Natalie said as she smoothed the creamy material over her body. It was tight. A week after they had gotten back from meeting her mom, she had found the garbage bag with her first wedding dress in. It was still moist, muddy, and by then, moldy. She had left it in the bag and sent it out with the trash. She, Mia, and Hazel had gone looking for another dress around Christmas and had found this one. It fit, and it was gorgeous. There was no train, and it was more form-fitting than the big puffy one she had forced out of the window months before.

Though it showed some of her scars, she didn't care anymore. Sam loved her scars. As for herself, she was working on not being so self-conscious of them. They were a part of her, a part that she couldn't forget, and now she didn't want to. The accident had changed her, and not just her body. It changed her from the selfish teenager to who she was today. Hazel had been right. The younger her could never have been a part of the book club. But to the older her, they were her best friends. And she couldn't see her life without them.

Suddenly the door flew open, and Hazel came rushing in and slammed the door shut behind her. Her blue dress was as tight-fitting as Natalie's white one was. No breathing for either of them today. Her short hair was styled with a single daisy in it, the same flower that was in the bouquets.

When she had started to plan the wedding, she had asked them all to be bridesmaids. Slowly they dropped out—Ruth because she was pregnant, Tess because she had a baby, Mandy had said she wasn't comfortable in a dress in front of everybody, and Mia had begged to be her personal attendant instead—which had left Hazel and Hazel alone. But it was perfect. It was to be Hazel the entire time. Just Hazel.

Over the months, Natalie had been able to let go of most of the guilt about surviving the accident. There would always be some guilt over it, but it was manageable, and she had been able to think about the twins with less pain than she had in the past. So far, she hadn't looked at a lot of the videos her dad had made, but sometimes she just needed to see her friends again. Just for a few minutes.

"Has she left yet?" Hazel asked Mia with a grin and then looked at Natalie. "Oh, she's still here."

"Thanks, Haze," she replied, smiling at her friend.

She was back as her friend. They may still not be in the same place regarding the accident, but they were both willing to admit they didn't have to be.

"Hey, it's not me. You have a reputation in this town."

Mia handed her the bottle. "Have a drink, Haze. She's staying. Apparently, this one is way better than the last one."

Taking the bottle, Hazel said, "I could have told you that. Anyone was better than that guy."

"I get your point, you two. Nobody liked Jason. But would you tell me if you even liked Sam?" Natalie took the bottle from Hazel and took another drink.

"We all love Mr. Sullivan." Hazel grinned.

"Can you call him Sam?" Natalie asked.

Hazel still usually called him Mr. Sullivan, which was the only time it ever felt creepy that they were getting married. Maybe when she was Mrs. Sullivan, it would be less creepy that he was Mr. Sullivan.

"Sexy Sam?" Hazel wiggled her eyebrow. "Do you remember when we made that one up?"

Natalie shot her a look. "Do you remember who said it first? I can't remember."

"Really? You did. You had the hots for him from the first moment you saw him. I should have known you would snag him. Just surprised it took so long." Hazel stepped away from the door as someone tried to open it.

The three other members of the group shoved into the little room, filling it. The three new arrivals gave Natalie hugs, and even Hazel got a few, along with compliments on her dress.

"So here we are again, Natalie's wedding. Seems like we do this every few months," Ruth joked as she leaned against the table near Mia, everyone loving a good wedding joke at her expense.

"I know, right. What do you think she'll do with the next one?" Tess asked and laughed.

"Very funny," Natalie said to them, but she was laughing as she said it. Nothing was getting her down about today. She was getting married.

"Mandy, grab the glasses." Mia pointed at the shelf. There was already a tray of twelve shot glasses.

"Why so many, Mia? Are we getting company?" Mandy asked, pulling the tray out and handing it to her cousin.

"No, I decided that everyone should get their choice of beverage. And since I don't know who is possibly pregnant, except Ruth, I just did one of everything for each," Mia said about their last celebration.

Mandy laughed and questioned her cousin's idea. "But why did you make an option for you? Do you think you're pregnant?"

"Shut up, Mandy, I wasn't thinking about that. Just two for all, and we are six, which equals twelve. Just to prove I am not, I will drink all the extra. No way am I pregnant." Her anger was getting the best of her.

"Mia, settle down." Ruth gave her friend a look of annoyance.

"Fine." Mia pushed away from Ruth, managing to hold the tray upright, a waitress to the core. "Everyone, take the drink of your choice, or two if you want."

Once everyone had chosen a glass, Mia put the tray back on the shelf behind her.

Natalie looked at her friends. They were there for her when she didn't get married and were now there for when she would. No questions asked, just being there for her. "I will make the toast; it's my wedding." Natalie lifted her glass and watched as everyone did. "I just want to say that book club has changed my life. You guys have changed my life. You are my best friends, and I don't want to know what life is like without you guys. To me!"

As she drank her tiny shot of whiskey, she watched her friends do the same. They all had tears in their eyes. Natalie knew that they all felt the same way. How had she even happened upon this group of women?

A knock on the door had all of them turning to look, each as guilty as the next for drinking in the church. Mandy was closest to the door and, with a shrug, opened it. After all, what could be done to them? They were all adults. Adults who probably knew better than to drink in a church.

To her surprise, Della Hart walked into the room, or squeezed into the room. It seemed everyone was aware of who she was, and they started to leave, each handing their empty glass to Mia as they walked past her. When everyone was gone, Mia set the stack on the table and silently walked out of the room.

Once it was empty, Della looked Natalie over and said, "You look gorgeous, Natalie."

"Thank you. I feel gorgeous. Do you think Sam will like it?" Looking down at her dress, she hadn't really thought about him liking it. She had liked it, and that was what was important.

"Sam likes you in everything." Della smiled at her.

It was true.

"Or nothing," Natalie said under her breath and then blushed feverishly. She had not just said that in front of her mother.

"So true." Della just laughed. "Those were your friends?"

"Yes, the book club." Natalie had told her about the book club. Well, not everything. What happens at book club stays at book club. In fact, she hadn't even told Sam yet everything that happened. But the rule was you couldn't tell until you were married, so maybe tonight. But she was sure they would be busy tonight.

"They seem nice," Della said.

"They're the best. Did you want a drink?" Natalie pulled the tray off the shelf. Someone had to drink them, and maybe there were more whiskeys than Mia should drink. Della looked down at the tray and up at Natalie. "Some are not whiskey if you're not partaking in alcohol."

Natalie took another glass and watched as her mom took one also. With a raised glass, they drank them. "Thank you for coming, Della. It was nice that you made the long trip here. You didn't have to. But I really wanted you here. Today I feel everything is perfect."

"There was nothing that could have kept me away. My baby girl is getting married, and I get to be here." Della hugged her, and Natalie couldn't see over the other woman's head today.

"How high are your heels?" Natalie had to know.

"Almost too high, but I knew you would be in heels and are already so tall. I didn't want to seem too short," Della said with a chuckle, looking at her feet.

"No heels for me. Sam said no since I'm almost as tall as him as it is. So, he got me these." She lifted her dress and showed her mom the new orange tennis shoes that matched her coaching ones.

"Orange? But it's supposed to be something blue." Della laughed at the shoes.

"Not when you're a Tiger, Mom." Natalie stopped. She had never called her that. They had never even talked about it.

"It makes me happy that you are comfortable enough to call me that. I know you had a mom you loved and you miss, but I feel honored to be your mom. Not just today, but every day. I regretted every day that I gave you up for adoption. That was until I met you and your dad. I couldn't ask for a better parent than him, and I assume your real mom was just as amazing. Because of them, you are amazing." Della hugged her again.

A knock interrupted their hug, and Hazel stuck her head into the room. "If you are going to do this, Natalie, you better get going. You're already late."

"Shut up, Haze." Natalie dabbed her tears away as Della took a step back.

Della gave her one last look. "I will go. Is your dad walking you down the aisle?"

"No, I am taking these last few steps alone," Natalie admitted, something she hadn't felt at her last wedding. But since that day, she had grown enough that she needed to stand alone for one last moment before she became one with Sam.

Della left to take her seat. Her mom. The last time she was here, she wished she had her mom there, and now she was. Turning to Hazel, she gave her a hug. She had wanted her as a bridesmaid, and she was. This was her perfect wedding. And she was getting to marry Sam.

Over the last few months, she had realized that nothing would change when they got married. They were still going to live together, sleep together, and do everything together. But she wanted to be married to Sam. In fact, she wasn't overly excited for the wedding, but everything that came after the wedding was what she was looking forward to this time around. The happily ever after.

CHAPTER 29

"She isn't coming," his brother Seth whispered from beside him when his bride was five minutes late.

Though the words should have freaked him out, he knew Natalie wouldn't take off. Not today.

Right now, he was wondering what Jason had thought when she had run off on him. Could he believe it either? He probably couldn't.

"She's coming," Pastor Ruston said behind him, though Sam saw nothing through the crack in the door to the sanctuary.

It didn't help that half the faces in the church were looking right at him, thinking she had left again. Once a runaway bride, always a runaway bride. Isn't that a saying? It felt like a saying—a bad one.

He might be starting to worry. Not about her standing him up at the altar, but her not being in his life anymore. What would he do if she wasn't in his life anymore?

"I thought for sure she would show up for you, Sam." His brother couldn't not chuckle as he whispered the words while they both stared at the closed door that she would walk through.

"Last time, all the bridesmaids were at the altar before the announcement was made," Ruston stated, as if that made him feel better about being abandoned.

The door swished open slowly, and all heads turned to see Hazel, except it wasn't Hazel. It was Mia's mother, Mrs. Lawson, sneaking in late, followed closely by her red-faced husband. But behind them, Sam could see blonde-haired Hazel in a pale blue dress with Mia doing something to her dress. The bride was nowhere in sight.

Once the couple was seated, the doors opened once more, and this time the music started to play a light and airy song that he had never heard before but was sure that Natalie had spent months thinking about.

So, he should have paid more attention to her wedding plans, now he could see that. But at the time, it was something that took her mind off the ending of the volleyball season and the adoption process that was a headache. Instead, he pushed the wedding on her, saying yes every time she asked him about something.

Now he had no idea what he'd said yes to, just that in the end, he got to marry Natalie Hart Beckett. It was all he wanted. In fact, he would marry her in a dirt field if that was what she wanted. But she wanted the church, the same church, and the same everyone here.

Hazel walked excruciatingly slow, and there was nothing that was going to rush her. Today he looked at the woman and didn't see her sister in her. Not anymore. Hazel had grown up where her sister hadn't had the opportunity. From the first time he had met the twins, he could tell them apart. There was just something that made them each unique. After the accident, Hazel lost that, but over the last few months, she had started to gain it back. She was becoming who she was again.

Her eyes met his, and she smiled, dimples and all. It was the same smile she had started giving him months ago, usually followed by asking why he put up with Natalie. Smiling back at her, he had recently started asking her the same thing. Their friendship had grown slowly but steadily until the pain of their shared loss was dulled.

As she got to the front of the church, she and Ruston exchanged a look, and Sam let his eyes look back at the double doors. Everyone was now looking at those doors, waiting for them to open.

When the wedding march started, the entire room got to their feet and turned toward the closed doors. He knew that Mia was making her perfect, except she was already perfect, and nothing Mia did in a few minutes would change that.

When the doors still didn't open, his brother leaned over to him and whispered, "Do you think she will marry the next guy?"

He nearly slugged his brother, except someone had grabbed his hand, stopping him. Turning at the touch he recognized, he stopped breathing when he saw Natalie in an off-white low-cut wedding dress that fit her like a glove. Better than a glove.

Before he could do anything, she leaned into him and kissed his shocked lips, her hands slipping under his tux jacket and pulling him close. He kept kissing her until he felt Ruston rest his hand on his shoulder. Stopping Sam instantly. It was only then that he heard the laughter coming from the guests and the wedding party.

Pulling away, he looked at his bride, who was just grinning at him. It seemed that she was not over playing tricks on him. And he knew he would happily put up with it for the rest of his life. At least he would once they were married.

"I didn't want to wait and needed to kiss you desperately, sexy Sam," she whispered as beside her, Hazel groaned loud enough for him to hear. Then she whined, "And the kiss isn't until the end."

"There isn't going to be an end, Natalie. This is forever." Taking her hand, he knew it would be the last time he saw it without his ring on it. He felt lucky that he was here, that he was the one who was marrying her, that they had come so close to missing this moment. He was glad he was the one who caught her that day and was able to be a part of her adventure.

"I like the sound of that." She leaned toward him, and he knew she was going to kiss him again.

"Dearly beloved, we are gathered here together ..." Ruston's voice got everyone's attention and stopped her movements instantly.

Once the vows were said, Sam was able to give Natalie the kiss she had been looking forward to, the kiss that would bind them forever. It was not nearly as special as the one she gave him minutes before when they were nearly alone in the full church, but it was just as important.

Turning to leave the church, he saw all the people who had come to celebrate this moment with them. There were a lot of them.

"So, how long until we're alone?" He took her hand in his as he whispered.

"Hours, maybe six or eight." She smiled and squeezed his hand, feeling the ring she had so recently placed there. The one she had 'borrowed' from her dad to go with her 'borrowed' one. From the moment she had seen Sam's grandmother's ring, she knew that it would match her dad's perfectly. It did, and now they were a set.

Walking down the aisle, he gave a pained expression and suggested, "Maybe we can sneak out of here and be alone a lot sooner."

Natalie laughed. "A runaway bride and groom? I like the sound of that."

"Me too, Mrs. Sullivan." He picked her up in his arms and headed down the aisle, just like he carried her to his pickup months before.

"I think I'm rubbing off on you, sexy Sam." She squealed and grabbed his neck as the church started to laugh with them.

EPILOGUE

THE WEATHERMAN HAD PROMISED RAIN, but Natalie was excited to see the morning sun peeking out from behind the clouds. In her dreams, this day was always sunny. Today her dreams were coming true.

Today her son was starting kindergarten in Landstad, North Dakota, with Hazel's son. To her excitement, the kids that were starting school today were John Henry and the boy that Natalie and Sam were in the process of adopting.

Actually, they were adopting two boys, a five-year-old and a three-year-old. Natalie had told Sam that she had wanted to start the adoption process as soon as possible, which meant soon after they became engaged, knowing it might take years. They had even gone through the same company Natalie had been adopted through years before.

By the summer after they got married, they had gotten word of brothers who needed a home. Milo and Theo had joined them within a few weeks, changing their lives completely. Natalie had known it was meant to be when one of the boys was only a few days younger than John Henry. It was like she and Hazel would have twins. Not that anyone would ever think of them as similar since John Henry was blond-haired and blue-eyed, and Natalie's Milo was dark-skinned with black hair and brown eyes. But the boys got along as well as she had with the twins at that age.

Natalie had decided that they would walk to school the first day, but tomorrow they would drive as a family. Today Sam would drop off Theo at the sitter and drive on to the school. Tomorrow they would drop him off together and take Milo to his second day of kindergarten.

At the corner that she had told Hazel they would meet on to walk the boys to school, Natalie and Milo stopped. But today was for Hazel and their boys starting a tradition.

Biting her lip, she wondered if she had pushed Hazel too much again. Usually, Hazel would point out that she was being too pushy, but sometimes not. Natalie had really been trying to reign it in, but sometimes Hazel needed the push.

"John Henry," Milo called and danced a little. Her son was super excited to start school. Grabbing his red backpack to keep him from running to his friend, she waved at Hazel with her other hand.

But Hazel hadn't been able to grab John Henry in time, and he came toward them at top speed. Once he was close enough, Natalie let go of the backpack, and the boys met a few feet away, already chatting.

As the boys talked, Natalie waited for Hazel to walk to them, but she didn't pick up speed at all. Watching her friend, she let herself think about Hanna and Henry for a moment. Natalie thought about them every day, but the pain that had been there for years was not there. She was now at peace with the friends who were gone, and her guilt was also mostly gone. The fact that she lived that day would always leave her with a little guilt, and she knew that Hazel would carry guilt too.

Once Hazel got near enough, Natalie gave her a hug. Hazel returned the hug willingly. It had taken time for her to respond to the hugs Natalie started to give her. "Can you believe we're walking our kids to school already?"

Hazel chuckled at her. "No. Once you set your mind to something, there's no stopping you."

"Hey, I just decided to adopt some kids, and one the perfect age just dropped into my lap." She turned to follow the boys down the sidewalk.

"Seems pretty fishy to me," Hazel replied.

"I love that they get along so well." Ignoring her, she nodded at the boys walking a few feet in front of them.

Hazel sighed. "I do too."

"How about we do this again in another five years?" Natalie asked.

"Then they'll be in the fourth grade," Hazel pointed out.

"I mean with another set of them. Kindergarten again. Maybe girls this time."

Hazel stopped and turned toward her, "No, because I do all the hard work of having a kid, and you just go out and find one. You always cheat."

"Not this time, Haze. This time I will have to go through all the hard work." Natalie hugged her again. "Sam and I are expecting."

"Congratulations, Natalie."

"Thank you, Hazel. But now you have to get pregnant too. We need to do this together," Natalie insisted in her whiny voice that always got to Hazel.

Natalie knew she was telling her friend way too soon since she was only a few weeks along. But she had always dreamed that their kids would be close in age.

"Are you telling me to get knocked up because you are?" Hazel demanded.

"Yes, let's do it together this time. It'll be so much fun!" Natalie put her arm around her friend.

"No. How does Sam even put up with you?" Hazel pushed the arm off.

"He loves me, so he does." Natalie laughed at her expression as the school came into view.

"I wonder how often he regrets that?" Hazel said under her breath.

"Never, Hazel May. Never."

After all these years, she loved having Hazel back in her life. Over the years, she hadn't even realized what she had been missing by not having her so close. And she knew that if she had married Jason that July day two years before, she never would have had her back in her life.

Watching Milo run into Sam's arms near the elementary wing of the school, she smiled at the scene. Sam was a great father, and she couldn't ask for a better husband. Everything he did was for his family.

"And you will always be crazy, Natalie. Now I have to go get some pictures of my son on his first day of school." Hazel walked away, taking her son's hand and leading him into the building.

"Mom, Dad is here!" Milo yelled at her in case Natalie could possibly miss the gorgeous man standing next to her son.

"I see that, Milo. Hello, Mr. Sullivan." She grinned at him. "Ready for another year?"

"It will never be as good as the first one, but I am ready. Are you ready, Mrs. Sullivan?" He took Milo's hand and they walked him into the school.

"It's just a library, Sam," Natalie said. Today was her first day as the school librarian. She had taken the job and turned in her notice at the city library in the spring and spent the summer with the boys and Sam. There had been many trips to his parents' cabin and to visit her mom's family. Since she had met them, she had learned that she may not look like them, but she acted just like them.

"Your dad has the video camera ready." Sam pointed out Patrick, who was recording the entire hallway around them, including a few seconds longer on John Henry than any others.

"He is awful with that thing. He must have already taken loads of their boys." Natalie loved having stepbrothers, especially because she never had to live with them. But she still wished that her dad had married Faith years. So many wasted years.

"Saves me from even bringing a camera." Sam pulled her to him as Milo ran off to his grandfather to get his locker in a video.

"One day, they will appreciate these tapes," Natalie said, thinking of all her tapes, most she hadn't even made it through yet.

Natalie watched her dad recording the images of her son's first day of school, catching every little thing. Who was going to be important to her son next year, in ten years, in twenty? Who was the face he'll be happy he sees in all the videos? Will there be some that are so painful he won't even be able to watch?

Ever so quietly, Natalie whispered, "Look, Mom. Look what Milo is doing today."

The End

Take a step away from the book club for non-book club member and sister to Mathias and Amanda Nordskov, Kit Kittson as she hides her true self from a playboy co-worker in <u>Intriguing</u>.

ALSO BY ALIE GARNETT

<u>Indulge</u>
Craving Winter
Enticing Aurora

<u>Landstad, ND</u>
Invisible
Irresistible
Impulsive
Insuppressible
Intriguing
Imperfect
Irreplaceable

<u>The Great Lovely Falls</u>
Falling for the Single Mom
Falling for his Best Friends Sister
Falling for the Boss
Falling for his Step-Sister
Falling for his Fake Wife
Falling into a Second Chance

<u>Hart Series</u>
Seeing her Pain
Her Favor
Max Valentine is Looking at Me!
Keeping her Safe

<u>Stand Alone</u>

Romancing the Doctor

ABOUT THE AUTHOR

I love to read and prefer a little spice in those books. I am lucky enough to live on a small hobby farm in northern Minnesota with her husband and two kids. I enjoy spending time in the pasture with my two mini horses and one fainting goat (who doesn't actually faint). When I'm not writing, I'm busy trying to do all the things I didn't get to while writing. Or maybe I wouldn't have gotten to them anyway, because its laundry, dishes and fun things like that.